CLIQUE
HERE

Also by Anna Staniszewski

Secondhand Wishes

Once Upon a Cruise

CLIQUE HERE

Anna Staniszewski

SCHOLASTIC INC.
NEW YORK

All rights reserved. Published by Scholastic Inc., *Publishers since 1920*. SCHOLASTIC and associated logos are trademarks and/ or registered trademarks of Scholastic Inc.

The publisher does not have any control over and does not assume any responsibility for author or third-party websites or their content.

This book is a work of fiction. Names, characters, places, and incidents are either the product of the author's imagination or are used fictitiously, and any resemblance to actual persons, living or dead, business establishments, events, or locales is entirely coincidental.

ISBN 978-1-338-68027-0

10 9 8 7 6 5 4 3 2   21 22 23 24 25

Printed in the U.S.A.   40
First printing 2021

Book design by Yaffa Jaskoll

"Bad times have a scientific value. These are occasions a good learner would not miss."
—Ralph Waldo Emerson

CLIQUE HERE

CHAPTER 1

There are eleven days until seventh grade starts, and I am *not* letting myself freak out. Instead, I invite my best friend over for an emergency slime-making session. Nothing calms me down like, as Kat calls it, "doing science."

"Lincoln will definitely be better than Hemlock," I say for the fifth time that afternoon. "I'm *totally* making the right decision."

Kat looks up from her spot at my kitchen counter, where she's been sketching out ideas for her newest batch of food-inspired superheroes. "Yes, Lily," she says with a groan.

"It's bigger, it has a ton more clubs and sports teams, and it's coed," I go on, pretty much reciting the presentation I gave my parents last spring when I was trying to convince them to let me change schools.

"And most importantly," Kat chimes in, "it does *not* have Queen Courtenay."

I nod. She's right. But after years of being singled out by Courtenay Lyons and her minions at Hemlock Academy, a fresh start at Lincoln Middle School sounds too good to be true. A place where no one cares that I do science experiments for fun and that my family isn't rich and that I'm nothing like my sister. A place where maybe I could even work up the courage to try out for soccer again.

"What do you think?" Kat asks, snapping me out of my thoughts. "Should Tater Tot shoot ketchup out of his eyes or out of his fingers?"

"Why not his ears?" I joke. "It would be like he has tomato-y earwax."

Kat chuckles. "Perfect!" She hunches over her sketchbook again and starts drawing furiously, her rainbow-streaked black hair falling in her eyes.

"You can always count on me for good ideas," I say.

I adjust the lime-green safety glasses that Kat got

me for my twelfth birthday and grab a box of baking soda. Then I sprinkle a half teaspoon into the shaving cream, Elmer's glue, and food coloring that I already combined in a bowl. That done, I squeeze in three tablespoons of my mom's contact lens solution—I'll have to remember to add it to the shopping list so I don't get in trouble for using so much again—and mix everything together. The pale blue concoction slowly stops sticking to the bowl and starts sticking to itself. I lift the spatula and the slime squelches in a way that's vaguely gastrointestinal.

Kat scrunches her nose as she glances over at the bowl. "That sounds so gross."

"It sounds like *chemistry*." There is nothing more satisfying than combining ingredients and creating a whole new substance.

"Just more proof that art is better than science," Kat says with a grin.

I snort. "Keep dreaming!"

This little argument has been going on between us for pretty much as long as we've been friends. Of course, at Hemlock Academy, neither art nor science is a winner. All that matters is being rich and pretty and—judging by Queen Courtenay—100 percent pure evil.

I give the slime another stir. The new formula I'm testing out seems frothier and less adhesive than ones I've tried before. I pull my trusty notebook and combination pen/screwdriver/ruler/level out of my pocket and flip through my notes on past experiments. When I come to a clean page, I jot down the results.

Light footsteps echo on the stairs. A moment later, my older sister, Maisie, practically bounces into the kitchen. She's wearing an outfit you'd expect to see on a toddler—a sparkly purple T-shirt and denim overalls—and there's glitter sprinkled in her hair. On any other almost-high-school-freshman it would look ridiculous, but it perfectly fits her upbeat personality.

"Hey, guys!" she chirps. Then she spots my bowl. "Uh-oh. *Someone's* stressed out!"

My sister knows me too well. "Not stressed, exactly," I insist. "I'm just—"

"Totally freaking out about changing schools," Kat cuts in.

"Hey!" I cry. Although maybe it's a tiny bit true.

"Aww, you'll be fine," Maisie assures me. "I know it's weird for both of us to be leaving Hemlock, but we can start over together, okay?"

Right, except that our situations are totally different. I'm slinking off to public school with my tail tucked between my legs while Maisie's practically riding off to St. Mary's, her new private high school, on a parade float. Courtenay might be the feared queen of my grade, but Maisie has been the adored mayor of Hemlock Academy since we were little. I don't think her "starting over" is going to be quite the same as mine.

"Besides," Maisie goes on, "no one at Lincoln knows you. This is your chance to show them who you really are."

"In that case, can I be Exploding Emma?" I ask.

Kat shakes her head. "I don't get why you're so obsessed with her. All she does is make stuff explode."

"Who are you guys talking about?" Maisie asks, her forehead crinkling.

"She's a YouTuber who does these cool chemistry

videos," I explain. "She's only sixteen and already a total science celebrity. I would kill to be her."

Maisie smiles. "Except you're you," she says, clearly not getting it. Then she peers into the bowl of slime. "That looks great, but you know what it could use?"

Kat and I look at each other. "Glitter?" we say in unison.

"Totally!" Maisie glances at her phone. "Oops, gotta go. I'm late meeting Ty for ice cream."

"Which one is Ty again?" I ask. My sister has so many friends that I've been thinking of putting them into a spreadsheet to keep track.

"I met him at one of Mom's fundraisers last year, remember? He gave me his number, so we've kept in touch." Only my sister would go to a charity event and come home with a guy's number.

"Is it like a date?" I ask.

Maisie laughs. "I don't know! I mean, he's cute, but he's just fun to hang out with, you know?" She slings her glittery bag over her shoulder. "Want me to bring a scoop of chocolate Oreo home for you, Lil?"

She really does know me too well. "Absolutely!"

"You got it! Tell Mom and Dad I'll be back for dinner, okay?" Then she rushes out of the house in a cloud of perfume and sparkles.

"One day I'm going to convince Maisie to donate her brain to science," I tell Kat. "There has to be some mysterious chemical that makes her so amazingly cheerful and nice all the time."

"Maybe it's all the glitter," Kat says.

I snort with laughter as I scribble a reminder in my notebook: *Research brain chemistry and "happy hormones."*

As I tuck my notebook away, I spot movement outside my kitchen window. Could it be? I squint toward the blue house three doors down, trying to get a better look. I can see the basketball hoop at the end of the driveway, but no one's using it.

"Lily?"

I almost drop my pen. "What?" I ask, pulling my eyes away from Parker Tanaka's house.

"Are you *still* stalking him?" Kat asks.

"No! Who?"

Kat rolls her eyes. "Why don't you just go *talk* to Parker?"

7

"No way! Remember what happened at the neighborhood block party last year?"

"So you froze up. No big deal," Kat says. "I bet he doesn't even remember."

But "froze up" doesn't cover it. When Parker said hi to me at the snack table, instead of saying something—anything—back to him, I stood there like a statue as my brain went into overdrive. *Should I say hi back? Should I introduce myself? But I already know his name. Does that mean he knows mine?* Thank goodness my sister came over and started chatting with Parker and his older sister so I could make a quick getaway.

I snatch up my spatula again and scrape the slime out of the bowl. "It's ready!" I announce. "Want to squeeze it and pretend it's Queen Courtenay's head?"

"Actually, I should get going," Kat says, packing up her sketchbook. "My mom thinks I'm going horseback riding this afternoon. I need to go home and set her straight."

"Is she *still* convinced you're doing equestrian?" I ask in disbelief. Every year, Kat's mom signs her up for the team. And every year, Kat doesn't attend a single practice or competition.

"You do have to admire her stubbornness," Kat says.

I smother a laugh. Kat might be adopted, but when it comes to being stubborn, she and her mom could be clones.

"Call me tonight?" I ask. "I need help figuring out the optimal first-day outfit."

"Lily, you still have over a week! And you'll be fine. This is what you wanted, remember?"

It's true. This *is* what I wanted.

"I just wish you were starting over with me," I say.

"And let Courtenay win? No way," Kat says. "I don't blame you for getting out, Lil, but I'm going to stay at Hemlock until the bitter end."

As I watch Kat bike away, I think about how years of being tortured by Queen Courtenay have affected the two of us in totally different ways. For example, in fifth grade, Queen Courtenay announced to everyone at lunch that Kat's birth parents in China must have taken one look at her and put her on a plane. The next morning, Kat showed up in her most blindingly colorful outfit, her hair newly streaked bright green, as if to prove how little Queen Courtenay's words had hurt her.

Meanwhile, I quit the soccer team in fourth grade because she made it so miserable, even though I'd been playing since kindergarten. And after "the incident" at the end-of-school dance last year, I decided I could never set foot at Hemlock again. That night, I made my "reasons I need to transfer" presentation, and the next week, my parents enrolled me at Lincoln.

I guess when it comes down to it, Queen Courtenay's torture has turned Kat into a lion and me into a mouse. I can't help wondering what we'd be like now if we could have just stayed ourselves.

An alarm beeps on my phone. Uh-oh. I need to clean up the kitchen counters or Mom will freak out when she comes home from work and there's nowhere to make dinner.

But as I start to turn away from the window, I notice someone at the end of Parker's driveway. My heart bounces in my chest as I dart across the kitchen to turn off the lights and then tiptoe back over to the window.

Parker is standing under the basketball hoop with a ball tucked under his arm. His skin glows golden against his Red Sox jersey and his dark hair hangs in his eyes in this totally adorable way. He is smiling so widely that his teeth gleam in the sunlight.

But who is he smiling at?

I press my nose to the windowpane and spot a girl on the sidewalk. She's casually leaning on what looks like a brand-new scooter. Her honey-blond hair is braided around her head in a sort of crown, and her white shorts and tank top somehow look casual and dressy at the same time. There's something familiar about her, although I'm pretty sure I've never seen her before.

The girl throws her head back and laughs, and suddenly I realize what it is. She has the same confident, effortless stance as Maisie and all the popular girls at Hemlock Academy, especially Queen Courtenay. No doubt, this girl and Parker are part of the popular crowd at Lincoln Middle School.

It's amazing that I can tell that simply by their clothes and their attitudes. All the elements are there, combined in the exact right ratio to make two perfect popular specimens.

As I stand there observing them—okay, fine, spying on them—I start to wonder: Are some people born to be popular? And if so, does that mean some of us are born to be outcasts?

CHAPTER 2

At breakfast the next morning, Mom and Maisie make plans to go back-to-school shopping at the outdoor mall a couple of towns over.

"Ooh!" Maisie says. "I should get a new outfit for Wyatt Campbell's end-of-summer pool party next weekend." My sister has attended more pool parties this summer than I have in my entire life.

They don't even bother inviting me shopping with them since I usually ask Mom to get me a few of the same pairs of pants and shirts in different colors. There's no point in fashion if you have to wear a uniform to school.

But at Lincoln, I won't be wearing a uniform. Which means that my clothes might be yet another thing that kids will make fun of me about.

"Can I come shopping too?" I ask.

Maisie's face lights up. "That would be so much fun!"

Mom looks surprised, but she says, "Maybe we could find you a couple of skirts or even sandals?" It's been her mission to get me into a skirt for years now.

"You know I can't wear open-toed shoes," I remind her. When I did my first junior scientist program at the Y years ago, one of the first rules I learned about being in a lab was that you always wear protective gear: long pants and sleeves, closed-toed shoes, safety goggles. Maybe I don't technically *need* to dress like that all the time, especially since my current lab is my kitchen counter, but I like feeling like I'm ready to "do science" at any moment.

"We'll find you some other cute stuff," Maisie assures me.

Just then, Dad shuffles into the kitchen to pour himself some coffee. Amazingly, he's already out of his pajamas and in what look like workout clothes.

"Joe and I are going for a run this morning," he announces.

"You're exercising with my brother?" Mom asks in disbelief. Dad's usual idea of working out is walking from the living room to the kitchen to get a snack. "What brought this on?"

Dad shrugs. "It sounded fun, that's all."

Maisie and I exchange a look. Whenever Uncle Joe is involved, there is never a simple explanation. He has this weird ability to talk Dad into anything.

Before any of us can push for an explanation, the doorbell rings and the front door opens.

"That must be Joe," Dad says.

"I didn't hear his car," I say. Uncle Joe has a ridiculous black convertible with one of those loud sporty engines that you can hear roaring down the street. He bought it right after he got his new job at a fancy law firm. Dad likes to make fun of him for owning a "gas guzzler," but I think he might also be a little jealous. Dad's had the same IT job at the local college and the same gray minivan for years.

"Good morning!" Uncle Joe calls from the hallway. When he comes into the kitchen, he flashes us a bright smile. He's wearing bike shorts and has a helmet tucked under his arm, looking like he stepped out of a fitness magazine.

"Did you *bike* over here?" Mom asks.

"It's a beautiful morning. I figured I'd go for it!" Uncle Joe says.

Dad's eyes widen. "That's got to be twenty miles!"

"Twenty-three, but it's a pretty easy ride," Uncle Joe says with a shrug. He turns to Dad. "Ready to go for that jog?"

Dad clears his throat. "Sure. I mean, if you're not too tired from all that biking."

"Not at all," Uncle Joe says. "Have to get in shape for our big race, right?"

"What race?" Mom asks.

Uncle Joe looks at her in surprise. "Didn't Drew tell you?"

We all look at Dad, whose cheeks are suddenly pink. "Oh, I thought I mentioned it."

"Drew and I signed up for a half marathon in October," Uncle Joe explains. "We'll be helping raise money for cancer research."

"Wow, honey," Mom says, clearly choosing her

words carefully. "It's a great cause, but October sounds . . . soon."

"Did your doctor say it was okay?" I ask.

Dad blinks at me. "Why wouldn't it be?"

"Well, thirteen miles is a lot if you aren't ready for it." That's basic science. Muscles have their limits. "I watched a video about marathon training once. It takes months, sometimes even years, to get ready for a race."

Dad's face pales. "Years? You didn't mention that, Joe."

"We'll be fine," Uncle Joe insists. "We have almost two months. That's plenty of time." Which is easy for him to say, considering that he thinks biking almost fifty miles in a day is no sweat.

Maisie, of course, is trying to be supportive. "If you ever want to come running with me, Dad, let me know!" She's been doing a bunch of training over the summer to get ready for the field hockey season.

He smiles. "Thanks, Mais."

Uncle Joe refills his water bottle and heads to the back door. "Ready to go, Drew?"

"Um, sure," Dad says, sounding anything but.

After the two of them leave, Maisie and I both crack up.

"At least Uncle Joe's not talking Dad into growing a beard again," Maisie says through her giggles.

"I don't know. I kind of liked the gnome look."

"Now, girls," Mom says. "We shouldn't make fun of your dad. It's not easy keeping up with my brother. I should know. I grew up with him!" But even she's smiling. Then she glances at the clock. "Okay, if we're going shopping, then we should get ready."

"We won't be there too long, right?" I ask. "Because there's this cool thing I saw online that I wanted to try today. You take milk and vinegar and turn it into plastic. The vinegar breaks down the proteins in the milk and then you squeeze out all the liquid and . . ."

I trail off as Mom gives me a blank stare. That's how she always reacts when I talk about my "science-y stuff," which she claims goes over her head. I know chemistry isn't really her thing, but it would be nice if she at least tried to act interested once in a while.

"Never mind," I say, and follow Maisie upstairs to get ready.

An hour later, we've joined a throng of back-to-school shoppers milling around the outdoor mall under a scalding August sun. Two minutes in and I'm already sweating. Last time I was here, it was the middle of winter and we ran from store to store to avoid freezing to death. I'm not sure who decided an outdoor mall in New England was a good idea, but they clearly never considered how incompatible it was with the average human's body temperature.

When we walk into the first store, I realize that I don't know anything about picking out clothes. Hemlock was a nightmare most of the time, but I actually liked having to wear a uniform every day.

My sister, of course, is in her element as she starts pulling items off the racks and inspecting them.

"Hey, Maisie? Do you think you could help me pick out a few things?" I ask finally.

Her face lights up like she's won the lottery. "Totally!"

She starts grabbing every glittery thing she sees, searching for the "right look" for me. But when I try on a few outfits she's picked out, they look terrible.

"Maybe we should start with some basics," Mom finally suggests.

"And then we can accessorize with sparkle," Maisie adds.

I nod, figuring they know what they're doing more than I do.

"You know, Lil," Mom says as we go back to flipping through racks, "maybe we should get your hair cut before school starts. Bangs might be cute?"

She tries to run her fingers through my hair, but I brush her hand away. "Bangs are harder to tie back, remember? I'd have to wear a hairnet during experiments." You'd never catch Exploding Emma with bangs.

Mom sighs. "Oh, Lil. You spend more time on making sludge in our kitchen than on caring for yourself."

"It's slime, not sludge."

"All I'm saying is that I'd love to see you put your

best foot forward at your new school. That way you won't have any problems this time."

Right, because it's *my* fault I was tortured by Queen Courtenay for years. If only I'd had bangs, she'd have left me alone.

The sad thing is, I know Mom really is trying to help. She just doesn't get it. Back when she was in school, she was like Maisie: adored by everyone, invited to every party, part of every club. She can't imagine what it's like to live life in my (closed-toed) shoes.

After we've picked out a couple of practical long-sleeved shirts for me, Maisie goes to try on bathing suits. It takes forever, of course, because they all look perfect on her. After a while, my stomach starts growling.

Thankfully, Mom takes pity on me. "Here," she says, handing me a few dollars. "Go get yourself a snack. We'll meet you at the shoe store in a few minutes."

I scamper away like a lab rat that's been set free. But as I head to a nearby sandwich shop, the worst possible thing happens: I spot Queen Courtenay.

She's perched at one of the outdoor tables, a poisonous spider waiting to trap me in her web.

I haven't seen her since the last day of sixth grade—right after the end-of-school dance, where she humiliated me in front of everyone. She hadn't made my life *easy* before then, but that night was like the catalyst that made the simmering solution of my life completely bubble over.

I told myself I was over it, that it wasn't a big deal. But suddenly I'm right back in the school gym, wearing a neon dress that Kat let me borrow, trying to shimmy along with her because "you have to dance at a dance." And then the sudden yank as someone pulled the zipper on the back of my dress. And the sensation of the dress sliding off me. And the cold horror of seeing my outfit around my ankles while I stood there in front of the entire gym in my underwear. Then, finally, grabbing my dress . . . pulling it up . . . running out of the gym . . . sobbing . . .

I blink, pushing the memory away. *I'm safe now. I'm okay.*

Queen Courtenay is with her entourage, of course: her two minions, who Kat and I always call Thing One and Thing Two because we can never tell them apart, and her ridiculously good-looking boyfriend, Brent, who goes to the all-boys school equivalent of Hemlock. I guess this is part of the chemical makeup of a middle school queen bee specimen.

Courtenay starts to turn my way, and my body unfreezes. I dive behind a nearby bench and duck down. I hold my breath, peering at her through the slats of the bench, terrified that she'll somehow sense that I'm here.

Finally she turns away from me. Phew. I should make a run for it, now while she's looking the other way. And yet, I can't seem to stop spying on her.

After a minute, Thing One brings out a milkshake for Courtenay. But when she goes to give it to the queen, Courtenay accidentally knocks it down and the milkshake splatters all over the place.

Courtenay jumps to her feet, screaming as if she'd been shot. "My shoes! It's on my shoes!"

The Things start scurrying around, mopping up her feet with napkins, while Brent dutifully goes back inside to get her another drink. Which is ridiculous since Courtenay is the one who spilled it in the first place.

The way they all move around her, the way they

hang on her every word and are scared of making her unhappy or angry, should disgust me. I know how she treats them is horrible and wrong. And yet . . . I also envy her. What would it be like to *be* her, to never have to be afraid?

I'm so deep in thought that I don't notice Courtenay leaving the table until it's too late. Suddenly she's walking right toward me, her entourage following her. There's nowhere for me to run.

I pop up, trying to pretend like I was admiring the bench and definitely NOT hiding behind it. And hoping that maybe she'll walk right past and not even recognize me.

But, of course, the instant she sees me, she stops. A smirk spreads across her face.

"What are *you* doing here, Flat Face?" It's the nickname she's had for me since fourth grade, for reasons I'm not sure I'll ever understand. (I even measured the contours of my face once, but they seemed to fall within normal parameters.) She used to taunt me with it on the soccer field when the coaches weren't paying attention.

Hydrogen, helium, lithium, beryllium, I start reciting in my head. It's something I've done ever since I was little, going through the periodic table of elements to calm myself down.

"Are you lost?" she asks when I don't answer, her perfect little nose wrinkled in disgust. "I thought you got all your clothes at the Salvation Army."

The Things titter with laughter while Brent stares at his phone, looking pretty checked out.

I try to move—I try to *run*! But my feet are frozen in place. *Boron, carbon, nitrogen, oxygen.*

"I heard you're not coming back to Hemlock this year," Courtenay goes on. "That's a shame."

For a second, I wonder how she knows. Then I remember that her dad is the assistant dean. He must have told her.

"I bet you think you can start all over at a new school, right? Like no one will notice what a loser you are." She snorts. "Yeah, good luck with that."

Then she walks past me, swinging a shopping bag in time with the swish of her ponytail. Her posse trails after her like a swarm of mosquitoes.

It takes me a good minute to unfreeze. And another for my breath to totally come back. On the outside, I'm cold and dizzy and shaking. But my insides are burning as hot as a thousand nuclear reactions.

My stomach is no longer growling with hunger. I just feel sick. So I stomp past the sandwich shop and start toward the shoe store where Mom and Maisie are probably waiting for me.

As I walk, I try to calm down. I try to breathe. *Fluorine, neon, sodium, magnesium.* I know Queen Courtenay is a horrible beast and I shouldn't listen to a word she says.

But the thing is, she's right. I thought I could start over, that I'd have a chance to hide at my new school and not get picked on. But the popular kids at Hemlock singled me out years ago, as if they could tell I wasn't one of them. What's to stop the exact same thing from happening when I go to Lincoln?

I need a way to protect myself. I can't deal with another "incident" again, one with zero consequences for the bully and all the consequences for me.

Because, as usual, Courtenay got away with it. No one

besides Kat was brave enough to come forward and say what really happened. So it was Kat's and my word against Courtenay's and her minions'. And her dad, of course, insisted that Courtenay would never attack another student. So Courtenay walked free while I went home and begged my parents to let me change schools.

No, I can't let something like that happen again. There has to be a way to really start over.

Gah. If only middle school were like slime. If only there were instructions that could tell you which clothes and friends and activities to combine in a bowl so that you could stir and stir until you became the exact right kind of person.

I stop walking, my brain swirling.

Wait. What if I *can* do that? That's what science is for—answering questions and attempting to solve the mysteries of the universe. If there was ever a scientific mystery, it's middle school popularity!

Okay, so the first step of the scientific process is easy: Ask a question.

I pull out my pen and notebook, and scrawl: *What makes someone popular?*

It sounds ridiculous. It sounds impossible. But then again, plenty of scientific discoveries seemed unimaginable until people figured them out.

Just then, I spot Mom and Maisie heading toward me, loaded up with shopping bags. "There you are," Mom says. "Are you ready to keep shopping?"

I open my mouth to tell her yes, but then I shut it again. Because I don't have enough information, do I? If I'm really going to do this, if I'm really going to figure out the inner workings of popularity, I'll have to take it step by step.

"Actually, I think I'm done for now," I say instead, tucking my notebook away in my pocket. "Maybe we could come back next week, though?"

In the meantime, I have some research to do.

CHAPTER 3

That night I open up a new spreadsheet and title it *Lily Blake Cooper's Popularity Experiment*. Then I enter in the scribbles from my notebook and start organizing the different fields. My body hums with excitement like it always does when I'm setting up a new experiment. I wonder if this is how Exploding Emma feels when she's working on her latest video.

I spend the rest of the weekend watching YouTube clips and listening to podcasts about the workings of popularity. I take quizzes online to find out *Why People Are Drawn to You!* and *Are You the Leader of the Pack?* Then, because I have to be thorough, I spend the next few days watching *Mean Girls* and *Grease* and anything else popularity-related that I can get my hands on.

My parents notice something is up because I'm suddenly poring over cheesy movies instead of watching Exploding Emma make rockets out of household items. But when I tell them that I'm trying to "research what life at public school is like," they seem to accept it. Mom is even kind of excited.

"Oh, I used to love this one!" she says, settling in on the couch next to me as I'm watching *10 Things I Hate About You*. "I always liked to imagine that I was the Bianca character."

Of course Mom *would* be the popular girl. I try to figure out which character I am and finally realize that I'm probably the nerdy boy who annoys everyone. Hmm.

Over the next few days, I plug my observations into the spreadsheet. I'm hoping to come up with a hypothesis so I can test it out. But there are so many popularity factors to consider: attitude, status, peer group. Not to mention the more superficial stuff like clothes and hair and accessories. The sheer scale of the project is starting to make me panic.

Finally, with only three days left before school starts and still no hypothesis, I decide to ask Kat for help. I probably should have brought her in earlier, but I was afraid she'd laugh at me. Or, worse, that she wouldn't understand.

Sure enough, the first thing she says when I call to explain my plan is "You don't need to change yourself for other people, Lily." But then she adds, "But if you do this, you should give yourself an alter ego."

I groan. "Not everything is a comic book, Kat!"

"No, hear me out. You need to separate your real self from your fictional self. That's what all super-heroes do."

Hmm. I'm not sure about that. But scientists *are* supposed to be objective. That's why they don't usually conduct experiments on themselves. Maybe creating a separate identity would help me be a little less biased about the results. Then it would be kind of like con-ducting the experiment on my alter ego rather than on myself.

"Okay, so what am I supposed to call myself? Popularity Girl?"

Kat chuckles. "Maybe a little too on the nose. Plus, it has to be a name you'll actually respond to."

That gives me an idea. "What if I went by my middle name? Blake?"

"Blake Cooper," Kat says thoughtfully. "It sounds like someone in a Disney movie."

"Um, is that a good thing?" I ask.

"For your purposes, I think it is."

But a new name is the least of my worries. "What I really need is some more field research," I say. "That will help me come up with a theory to test out." I have plenty of data from my interactions with Queen Courtenay, but those are all about getting picked on by the popular kids. What I need are more opportunities like the one I had to spy on her at the mall so I can observe how to *be* one of the popular kids.

After Kat and I hang up, Maisie knocks on my door. She's wearing her new sparkly bathing suit with a pair of shorts. "Hey, can you tie this for me?" she asks, holding up the straps of her bikini top. "I can never do that fancy knot you do."

"It's a simple square knot," I say, getting up to help her. "Whose party are you going to, again?"

"Wyatt Campbell's," she says. "It'll mostly be

Douglas High kids, so I won't know a lot of people, but it should be fun."

Only my sister would waltz into a party full of kids she didn't know and think it was fun. But I guess that's the thing about being popular. Somehow you always manage to find a crowd.

Wait. Maybe this is it. The research opportunity Kat and I were just talking about.

"Hey, Mais," I say. "Any chance I could come with you?"

"Wow, really?" Maisie says. A normal sibling would be annoyed that their younger sister wanted to tag along. But Maisie's face breaks into a smile. "Oh, it'll be so fun to have you there! This party is like my last hurrah."

"Because summer is ending, you mean?" I ask. But that doesn't make sense. Even during the school year, Maisie's always at some party or sleepover or field hockey game. It doesn't seem as though her social life ever slows down, no matter the season. My social life, on the other hand, has pretty much only consisted of hanging out with Kat and occasionally getting dragged to a family barbecue or one of Mom's fundraisers.

Maisie only shrugs and says, "Let's go see if Dad will drive us."

We go downstairs to find Dad sprawled on the couch, with an ice pack on his knee and a heating pad on his neck, recovering from his latest workout with Uncle Joe.

If Maisie was surprised I wanted to go to the pool party, Dad is downright shocked. "Lily, you're really going with Maisie? To a party? Is, um, is everything okay?"

He looks genuinely worried, like I might be having some sort of episode, so I decide to clue him in a tiny bit. "It's for research," I tell him, holding up my notebook.

"Oh." The lines around his eyes ease. This he can understand. I'm always researching one weird thing or another. Last summer it was the life cycle of fruit flies. It took weeks to get our kitchen bug-free again. "I hope you manage to have some fun while you're at it," he adds.

Thankfully Mom is working a charity event today. I can just imagine the endless pictures and the cooing if she saw her daughters leaving for a party together.

I go up to my room and dig one of Maisie's old bathing suits out of a musty storage bin in the back of my closet. It's a glittery tankini I would never dare wear normally because you can see a hint of my belly button. But if there's one thing I've learned from my research so far, it's that I have to look the part in order to blend in. So instead of wearing my usual jeans and sneakers, I keep digging through Maisie's hand-me-downs until I find a yellow skirt and flip-flops.

My legs and toes feel so exposed that I'm about to put on something else. But then Maisie comes into my room and squeals, "Wow, Lily. You look great!"

My sister has never reacted to me that way before, and I feel my cheeks go red. I tell myself that I *can* walk around with bare legs and toes for a couple of hours. We'll be by a pool, after all.

"Um, do you think you could help me with my hair?" I tried watching some hair tutorials to see if I could braid it the way that girl in Parker's driveway had hers. But my test run looked more like a bird's nest than a crown.

"Sure!" Maisie says. "What do you want me to do with it?"

"Maybe one of those slicked-back high-ponytail things?" I ask, thinking about my research and remembering Courtenay's hair when I saw her at the mall.

My sister nods excitedly. Then she attacks my unruly waves with some sort of spray that she says will "smooth down flyaways" (whatever that means) and starts brushing.

"I can't believe we're going to a party together, Lil," Maisie says. "You are going to love it!"

"Wait. I won't actually have to talk to anyone, will I?" I've been so focused on collecting more data that I forgot all about the socializing people do at parties.

"When in doubt, smile and nod," she says. "Always works for me!"

I nod slowly and flash her a nervous smile.

"See? You're a natural!" she chirps.

"Hey, um, do you think it would be weird if I changed my name to Blake?" I ask.

"Blake Cooper. That's adorable!"

"Um, thanks," I say. "So at the party, maybe you could try calling me that?"

"Sure thing!"

I really do have the best sister in the world.

Ten minutes later, Maisie is finished grooming me. She begs me to let her spray glitter in my hair, but I wave her away. I might be trying out a new persona, but I haven't completely lost my mind!

When I glance in the mirror, I don't look as effortlessly glamorous as my sister does, but I'm more polished than my usual Lily self. Hopefully that means I'm ready to be Blake.

CHAPTER 4

After Dad drops us off at the party, I follow Maisie up the walkway of Wyatt's house. I yank on the bottom of my skirt to make it cover more of my legs. As we get closer to the front door, the sounds of kids talking and laughing waft toward us, and my hands start shaking.

Hydrogen, helium, lithium . . .

Maisie must see that I'm starting to freak out because she says, "Don't worry. Everyone here is super nice." Then she loops her arm through mine and drags me inside.

The house is packed with kids who look so much older than me. Some of them probably drove here! I eye the plastic cups in their hands, wondering if there's beer in any of them. That's what happens at high school parties, right? At least in all those movies I've been watching recently. Don't they know teen drinking affects brain development??

When I spot a woman who's obviously Wyatt's mom handing him a plate loaded with snacks, I relax a little. Maybe this is a regular party that poses no immediate danger to underdeveloped brains.

Maisie drags me through the kitchen and living room, effortlessly chatting with everyone. "It's so nice to meet you" and "I think we chatted at Hailey's party last year" and "I love your sunglasses—so chic!"

It's amazing to watch. Even though my sister has to be one of the youngest people here besides me— she's going to be a freshman this year and Wyatt, I find out, is a rising senior—she fits right in. Like some sort of social chameleon who adapts to any environment. She doesn't even go to school with most of these kids, but that doesn't stop her from treating everyone like an old friend. It's so completely different from the way Courtenay treats people. But it seems to work for Maisie. Maybe it could work for me too?

I tag along after her, trying to smile and nod like

she told me to. I wish I'd brought my notebook to jot down my observations, but it wouldn't fit in the tiny pockets of my skirt. So I try to take good mental notes instead, remembering as many details as I can to put in my spreadsheet later.

But after a few minutes, my brain is bursting with information and my face feels ready to crack in half from all that smiling. When my sister suggests we go outside to say hi to people by the pool, I pretend I have to go use the bathroom. Then I sneak off to a corner of the empty sunroom to breathe.

I can't believe I'm really doing this. I'm at a high school party, and so far, no "you don't belong here" alarms have gone off.

As I wander around the room, a photograph on the wall catches my eye. It's some sort of brown pattern that makes me think of shingles on a house. I go over and study it up close, trying to put my finger on what it reminds me of.

"It's a snake," someone says.

I whirl around to find a boy about my age standing in the doorway. "Um, what?"

"The photograph. It's a close-up of the scales of a rattlesnake," the boy says. When he comes closer, I notice he's a little shorter than I am, with round pink cheeks and thick eyebrows. I smile at his T-shirt: It has the periodic table of elements and the words "I wear this shirt periodically" written underneath.

I glance back at the photo. "Wow, that's cool," I say.

"It was tough to get close enough to get a good picture," he says. "You know, rattlesnake venom and everything. But it was at the zoo, so I wasn't in *too* much danger." He chuckles.

"Wait, *you* took this?"

He shrugs. "Yeah, I like to photograph things up close, see what they look like."

"Huh. Have you ever done that through one of those fancy microscopes?" I ask.

The boy's face tightens. "I had one, but my older brother broke it. My parents said they'll make him buy me a new one, but considering he doesn't have a job, it's taking forever."

"That's a bummer," I say. "If it makes you feel any

better, my mom keeps saying she'll get me the crystal-growing kit that I wanted when I was eight. I'm still waiting."

He smiles, and it hits me that I'm actually doing it! I'm talking to a boy at a party!

"I'm Owen, by the way."

"Lil—um, Blake."

"Lil' Blake?" he repeats. "Is that your rapper name?"

"No," I say with a nervous laugh. "It's just Blake."

"Okay, Just Blake. So what brings you to this party?"

"I came with my sister. What about you?"

He gives me a funny look. "Well, Wyatt is my brother, so . . ."

Oh. Oh! Of course, that makes sense that Owen lives here. Why else would his stuff be hanging on the wall?

"Um . . . so you're really into photography?" I ask, desperate to change the subject.

Owen shrugs. "It's just for fun. Not what I want to do with my life or anything." He leans against one of the wicker couches. "Where do you go to school?"

"Um, I'm starting at Lincoln Middle this year. Seventh grade."

"Nice! I'll be in seventh there too. If you're into crystals and microscopes and stuff, we have an awesome science club." I must make a face because he adds, "I know it doesn't sound that great, but it's pretty platinum."

"Platinum?" I repeat.

"Yeah," he says with a little laugh. "Better than gold."

"That does sound pretty platinum," I admit. "My old school didn't have a science club." But as tempting as it is, I doubt that kind of club would fit into my popularity experiment. And really, should I even be standing around talking to a boy who is so obviously a nerd? A nice and kind-of-cute nerd, but still.

Just then, a girl comes into the sunroom. She's tall and skinny with wavy hair that's a few shades darker than her brown skin.

"Oh, speaking of the science club," Owen says, "this is Priya, the club president." The way he looks at her, his eyes full of awe, I get the feeling she might be a little more to him than that.

Priya gives me a distracted wave. "Yup, that's me." Then she turns to Owen. "You wanted my help with something?"

He glances at me. "Oh, yeah. Um . . ." Whatever it is, he clearly doesn't want to talk about it in front of me.

"I'm gonna go find my bathroom," I announce. Oops. "I mean the sister. I mean *the* bathroom and *my* sister!" My cheeks are suddenly on fire as I hurry out of the room.

"See you later, Lil' Blake," Owen calls after me as I flee to the safety of the kitchen.

My face is still burning hot, so I figure a soda might help cool me down. But as I head to the fridge, I spot someone in the living room. I know that floppy black hair and that confident swagger.

Oh my goodness. It's Parker Tanaka! What is he doing at this party?

I tiptoe forward to get a better look and find Parker by the TV talking to a girl I recognize as his older sister, Maya. He must have come with her.

"Why couldn't you drop me off at soccer practice

carly?" I hear him saying. "Instead of bringing me here?"

Maya rolls her eyes. "Because I'm not going to drive across town twice! Besides, you used to practically live at this house."

"Yeah, when I was a little kid," Parker says. "Owen and I don't really hang out anymore."

"Well, whatever. I told Wyatt I'd swing by, so stay here, okay?" Maya says. Then she goes out by the pool, leaving Parker alone. He sighs and slumps onto the couch, focusing on the Red Sox game on TV.

That's when it hits me. This is it. This is my chance to finally talk to him without making a complete fool out of myself!

My brain screams at me to run. Yes, talking to Owen was surprisingly easy and only a tiny bit disastrous, but this is Parker Tanaka. What am I even supposed to say to him? But then again, how amazing would it be to be able to tell Kat that I *have* in fact talked to Parker? Plus, this would give me so much more data to use in my experiment. I can't let this chance slip by.

Hydrogen, helium, lithium.

With my legs ready to buckle under me, I stumble to the couch and sit as far away from Parker as I can.

He glances over at me and smiles. "Hi," he says.

"Hydrogen!" I blurt out.

GAH!!!!

Parker blinks. "Um, what?"

Okay. I need to get it together. I can't mess this up!

I scramble for something to say, anything. "Wh-what's the score?"

Parker gives me a strange look. Then he points to the TV and reads the numbers on the screen. "Seven to six, Yankees," he says.

"Oh." I swallow. "D-does that mean we're winning? Or that they're winning? Or is it too soon in the game to tell? Is it even called a game or is it a match or . . ." Ah! Why can't I stop talking??

Parker chuckles. "Not a big baseball fan, huh?"

My cheeks are blazing again. "N-not really," I admit.

"No worries," Parker says, glancing at me again. "Hey, you live on my street, right?"

Oh no. He's probably remembering our last

catastrophic meeting at the neighborhood block party. I wait for him to make an excuse and hurry away, but he doesn't. Maybe Kat is right and he forgot!

He's looking at me expectantly, so I manage, "Um, yeah . . . I'm Lily." I cough. "I mean, that's my official name, but people call me Blake."

"Hi, Blake," he says. "I'm Parker." Then he gives me another dazzling smile and turns back to the game.

Does that mean our conversation is over? Now that we're actually talking to each other, I don't want it to end. "So . . . is baseball really hard to learn?" I try.

Parker shakes his head. "No, not really." He starts to tell me about innings and balls and strikes and intentional walks. It's clear how much he loves talking about the sport. He keeps his eyes on the game as he waves his hands around excitedly.

I barely focus on what he's saying, though, because all I can do is marvel at the fact that I'm sitting three feet away from him and that he's talking to me. Parker Tanaka is actually talking to me! Now that I'm up close to him (rather than spying on him from afar), I can see that his face is nearly perfectly symmetrical.

That explains why he's so cute. Biologically speaking, humans love symmetry.

I should try to find a way to casually bring up the fact that he and I will be at the same school this year. Maybe he'd even want to sit together on the bus!

"Anyway, sorry," Parker says. "I'm probably boring you with—"

"I'm transferring to Lincoln this year!" I blurt.

Parker's eyebrows shoot up. "Oh, wow. That's—"

"We'll be on the same bus!" Oh my gosh. What is *wrong* with me?

Before I can shout out anything else, a familiar shriek echoes behind us.

I turn to see Maisie standing in the kitchen, holding a bottle of lemonade that's spraying all over her. She drops it in the sink, but it's already completely soaked her.

"I—I have to go," I say to Parker, jumping to my feet. Then I hurry over to Maisie. "Are you okay?"

She nods, managing a laugh despite the fact that she's all sticky and wet and there's glitter dripping down her face.

"I don't know what happened," she says. "I was talking to Wyatt, and then he went back outside and I grabbed the lemonade and it exploded."

"Do you want me to get Dad to pick us up?" I ask. That's what I'd do in this situation: flee as quickly as possible.

But before she can answer a flock of girls flutter over, armed with paper towels and tissues and sympathy.

"Oh my goodness, are you okay?" one of them coos.

"Want me to find you some dry clothes?" another one offers.

"Oh, that's okay," Maisie says. "I'm fine. I just feel bad that the floor's such a mess!"

"No problem!" the first girl says. "I'll track down a mop." Then she rushes off.

Suddenly this all feels so oddly familiar. It's like when Queen Courtenay spilled her milkshake and the kids in her entourage were falling all over themselves to help her.

But Maisie doesn't even know these girls. She only met them a few minutes ago. Why would they help her? I've certainly never had strangers dying to help me, even when I could have used it.

I guess that's what it's like to be a popular girl like Maisie. She attracts people everywhere she goes. No matter what, she always has a posse. That's what keeps her safe.

Safe.

Something in my brain clicks, and suddenly I know exactly what my hypothesis will be.

CHAPTER 5

By the end of summer vacation, I've narrowed my research down to what I call the Five Factors of Popularity. Then I come up with specific goals to help me achieve these factors when I get to Lincoln.

FACTOR 1: ENTOURAGE

GOAL: I'M NOT DELUSIONAL ENOUGH TO THINK I COULD HAVE AN ENTOURAGE OF MY OWN, BUT I CAN AT LEAST BECOME A MINION TO ONE OF THE POPULAR GIRLS.

FACTOR 2: BOYFRIEND/GUY FRIEND

GOAL: A BOYFRIEND MIGHT BE TOO MUCH TO HOPE FOR AT THIS POINT, BUT I'LL SETTLE FOR A CUTE GUY FRIEND, PERHAPS ONE WHO LIVES ON MY STREET AND IS REALLY INTO BASEBALL . . .

FACTOR 3: SOCIAL LIFE

GOAL: I CAN'T JUST HANG OUT WITH KAT ALL THE TIME. I NEED TO START GOING TO PARTIES AND JOINING CLUBS—AND TRY TO ACTUALLY ENJOY IT!

FACTOR 4: ATTITUDE

GOAL: NO MATTER HOW MUCH I'M FREAKING OUT, I NEED TO ACT LIKE I'M SAFE AND COMFORTABLE ALL THE TIME.

FACTOR 5: APPEARANCE

GOAL: CUE THE MAKEOVER MONTAGE IN EVERY CHEESY TEEN MOVIE! OKAY, I'M NOT GOING TO GO OVERBOARD, BUT I DO NEED TO FIND A STYLE THAT MAKES ME FEEL MORE POLISHED AND CONFIDENT AND LESS . . . ME.

I read through the Five Factors over and over again. Entourage, Boyfriend/Guy Friend, Social Life, Attitude, and Appearance. Putting everything into one list makes my experiment feel a lot more concrete. Now I just need to find a way to make all five of these things happen at Lincoln. Easy, right? (Eek!)

The first day of school, I wake up earlier than I probably have in my entire life. If I really am going to do this, if I really am going to become Blake Cooper, I need time to prepare.

With Kat's help, I've managed to cobble together an outfit to wear. I'll have to get Mom to take me shopping again this weekend for more suitable clothes, but between my old stuff and some of Maisie's hand-me-downs, I should be able to make it through the next few days.

When I glance in the mirror, I see a Queen Courtenay wannabe staring back at me. The sight is terrifying . . . but also kind of exactly what I was going for. Appearance? Check!

When I go downstairs for breakfast, Dad actually spits out his coffee at the sight of me.

"Are you wearing a *skirt*?" Mom asks in disbelief. "And are those . . . *flip-flops*?" Her eyes might actually pop out of her head.

"Do I look okay?" I ask, feeling self-conscious all over again.

"You look great!" Maisie cries. And it really sounds like she means it. "I knew that outfit would be perfect!"

"Do you think you could do my hair again?" I ask. St. Mary's doesn't start school until tomorrow, so Maisie's still in her pajamas, not worrying about getting ready.

"Of course!" She rushes out, then hurries back to the kitchen with supplies.

"You knew about this little makeover?" Mom asks my sister.

Maisie shrugs as she brushes and spritzes. "Blake wanted my help, so I helped."

"Blake?" Mom and Dad say together.

I clear my throat. "Oh, um. Yeah. I figured, new school, new name. What do you think?"

Mom's the first one to recover from the shock. "Well, I mean . . . we named you Blake after my grandfather, so it's a lovely name. But . . ." She looks to Dad for help.

"What's wrong with Lily?" he asks.

"Nothing. I want to try something new, that's all." I turn to Mom. "You kept saying I should put my best foot forward, remember?"

"Well, yes." Mom gives me another look and then she smiles. "I seem to recall Maisie having a few make-overs in middle school too. Remember when you dyed your hair orange, Mais?"

"I think I was going for red," Maisie says.

Dad groans. "Don't give your sister any ideas!"

"I guess it's just something you girls need to go

through, right?" Mom gets up and kisses my cheek. "And you look lovely, Lily. Um, I mean Blake." She laughs. "The name's going to take some getting used to."

But Dad is still frowning. "There's nothing wrong with being yourself, you know," he says. "Don't do things simply because other people want you to." Which is hilarious considering he's the one killing himself to train for a half marathon he doesn't even want to do.

"I *am* being myself," I say. Just a scientifically improved version.

As I head over to the bus stop, I get a text from Kat. *Good luck, Blake!*

The fact that she's using my new name makes me a little less nervous. If Kat thinks I can do this, then maybe I really can.

Thanks, you too! I write, since it's also her first day back at Hemlock. Oh boy, do I wish we could be together. But I'll have to conduct research on my own. I go through the mental list of goals for my experiment. I've done my best with Appearance. Now it's on to Entourage. I need to identify the popular kids and find a way to minion-ize myself.

Since I've never taken the bus before, I accidentally get to the stop before anyone else. Then I stand there, waiting, for what feels like forever, trying to blend in with a nearby tree. Finally other kids start trickling over, but only a couple of them look familiar. I keep an eye out for Parker, determined to have a normal conversation with him this time. I even looked up some Red Sox stats to have something to talk about.

But when the bus arrives, there's still no sign of Parker. When I climb on, I survey the half-empty bus. All the popular kids are probably sitting in the back—isn't that how it works?—so I slide into one of the seats in the front, next to a girl who's staring out the window. I figure I'll lie low and observe until we get to school.

After I sit down, Parker rushes onto the bus, apologizing to the driver for being late. I try to give him a little wave as he hurries down the aisle, but he doesn't seem to notice me. I swallow down my disappointment as the bus pulls away.

The person next to me starts humming. I glance over at the girl and realize that I've seen her before. But where? Then I suck in a breath. Whoa. It's the girl I saw talking to Parker in his driveway the other day! What is she doing sitting up here?

"Hey," she says when she catches me staring at her. "I'm Ashleigh. Are you new?"

Based on everything I observed the other day, she has to be popular. Oh my gosh. A popular girl is talking to me!

My mouse instincts tell me, Scurry! and Retreat! But I force myself to smile and nod like Maisie taught me. Then I say, "Blake. Yes. Blake."

Her perfect smile fades slightly. "Are you saying your name is Blake?" she asks uncertainly.

I can feel the list of periodic elements trying to burst out of my mouth again. *No.* I can't lose it now!

Okay, ready or not, it's time for Factor 4: Attitude. I need to act as if talking to people is no big deal. As if this girl is a person, same as me.

Somehow, thinking of her as a fellow *Homo sapien* makes me feel a tiny bit less tongue-tied.

"Sorry, yeah. My name's Blake. It's my first day at Lincoln."

"Cool!" she says, her smile going back to full wattage. "Parker said we'd have a new girl on the bus."

I blush as I remember pretty much shouting that information at him the other day. But at least he remembered. That could be a good sign, right?

"He said you were at a pool party at Owen Campbell's house?" Ashleigh goes on. She crinkles her perfectly freckled nose, as if she's smelled something rotten. "You might want to stay away from Owen. He and Priya . . ." She doesn't finish, but it's obvious what she's saying. *Stay away from them because they're losers.*

My stomach squeezes with disappointment. But what did I expect, that because she's being nice to me, she wouldn't be as snotty and judgmental as the popular kids at Hemlock? Owen might be a nice guy, but he's also clearly a nerd. Of course someone like Ashleigh would stay as far away from him as possible.

"Thanks for the tip," I mumble.

"So did you just move here?" she asks.

I shake my head and explain how I'd gone to Hemlock since kindergarten.

"Oh, cool," she says. "I used to know someone who goes there. And we play against their soccer team sometimes. It seems like a pretty great school."

"Um, yeah. I guess. But I was ready for a change."

Ashleigh nods. "Sometimes I kind of wish I could start over at a new school too."

Whoa. Really? If I were one of the popular kids, I don't think I'd want to go anywhere.

"So are you into sports?" Ashleigh asks.

"Yeah, I play soccer," I find myself saying. "Or, at least, I *did*." Until Queen Courtenay decided it would be fun to see how many times she could kick the ball straight into my face during practice. I managed to survive a week of bloody noses before I finally quit the team.

Ashleigh's face lights up. "You should join the Lincoln team! It's so much fun. Parker plays too, since baseball isn't until the spring."

"Oh, I don't know. I'm pretty out of practice." Plus, I'm not sure I can handle being out on the field again.

It would bring back too many horrible memories.

"There aren't any tryouts," she says. "Everyone who wants to be on the team gets in. Coach Nazari doesn't really care about winning. We just do it because it's fun!"

That *does* sound kind of fun. And a lot different from the way things were at Hemlock. Even back in fourth grade, when the games didn't actually count for anything, the kids were all so competitive.

"Okay, maybe," I say, letting a small bubble of excitement well up inside me.

We pull up to the school and start filing off the bus. I catch Parker's eye, and he actually gives me a little nod! My stomach flutters as I manage to wave back at him.

"Find me at lunch?" Ashleigh asks as we head into the school.

"Sure!" I know I sound way too eager, but I can't help it. The school day hasn't even started yet and I've already managed to find a clearly popular girl who seems to think I'm minion material!

As Ashleigh heads down the hall, I grab my phone and send Kat a message. *It's working!!!*

My excitement fades, though, when a crowd of kids streams past me. There are strangers, complete strangers, everywhere. I knew Lincoln was a lot bigger than Hemlock, but I wasn't expecting *this*! The crowd sort of pushes me along until I find myself outside the main office, so overwhelmed that I can't even move.

"Um, excuse me?" someone says behind me.

Oops. I'm blocking the office door, so no one can get in or out.

"Sorry." I step aside and realize that the girl trying to get past is Owen's friend from the party. "Oh, you're Priya."

She purses her lips, as if trying to remember who I am. Then she says, "Right. Blake. Are you okay?"

"Yeah, fine. Sorry. It's my first day." As if that explains why I'm standing frozen in the hallway.

"Okay, come on," she says, waving for me to follow her into the office. That's when I notice her earrings.

"Whoa, are those double helixes?" I ask before I can stop myself.

She shrugs. "My parents got me them for my birthday."

62

"Wow! I asked my mom for beaded earrings that looked like beakers once, and she thought I was joking. You're so lucky your family actually understands you."

Priya doesn't answer. Instead, she leads me over to the desk, where an older man in a coffee-stained shirt asks for my name. He's a far cry from the snotty British lady who runs the main office at Hemlock Academy.

While he's typing away, Priya taps her foot impatiently. Finally she asks the man, "Can you do something for me real quick? I need a pass for lunch. Science club business."

My ears perk up at the words "science club." That's right. Priya's the president.

I expect the man to tell her to hold on, so I'm surprised when he stops typing and grabs a pad of paper and scribbles out a pass. "Anything for science club," he says with a smile as he hands it to her. Then he goes back to typing.

"Well, see ya," Priya says to me. Then she stops and seems to consider me for a moment. "I suppose you're looking for someone to sit with at lunch." It's a statement, not a question.

I almost tell her yes. Would it be so bad to give up my popularity plan and go be one of the science club kids? If Owen and Priya are any indication, I'd fit right in. They are my people, right? But . . . but being in science club won't give me the most important part of my plan. It won't keep me safe.

Besides, my experiment is already going so well. I can't give up on it now.

"Actually, I already have someone to sit with."

Priya shrugs. "Okay. Well, good luck." Then she heads off into the crowd, leaving me to navigate the halls on my own.

CHAPTER 6

The rest of the morning is a blur of identical hallways and unknown faces. I try to take as many notes in my notebook as I can, writing down where the obviously popular kids sit in each classroom, what they're wearing, and how they interact with one another. By the time I get to the cafeteria, I feel like I'm drowning in all the new people and observations. If only Kat were here, I wouldn't be so lost.

It takes me forever to find Ashleigh at lunch. I expect her to be sitting in the middle of the cafeteria, at the "nucleus table," as Kat and I called it at Hemlock—the one in the center of everything. But the tables here are arranged in uneven rows, so it's hard to tell where the center is. I wander past a line of recycling bins. At Hemlock, we had trash and recycling. Here there's landfill, plastics, papers, compost, etc. I'm kind of dreading the moment when I have to throw something away.

As I wander around the cafeteria, I notice Owen smiling at me from a table by the windows. Priya is right beside him. He lifts his hand, as if he's about to wave me over. Ack! I quickly turn away and pretend I don't see him. I feel awful blowing him off, but I have to find Ashleigh and stick with my plan. Otherwise, my experiment will be dead in the water.

Finally I spot her sitting at a table with Parker, a boy who looks far too huge to be in middle school, and a tiny girl with perfect red ringlets.

"Guys, this is Blake," Ashleigh says as I sit down next to her. "Blake, this is Hector and Jayla. And you know Parker."

"Hi, neighbor!" he says, flashing me a big smile.

Even though I'm vibrating with nervousness, I manage something like a smile back. Then I actually manage to answer the standard "Where did you move from?" and "What was Hemlock like?" questions without embarrassing myself. When the conversation moves to sports again, it turns out that Hector is really into wrestling. Considering he's a foot taller and wider than the average for kids our age, I'm sure he's great at it. Jayla, on the other hand, is a gymnast, dancer, and cheerleader.

I can't believe how nice they're all being to me. Maybe Lincoln isn't like Hemlock. Maybe at this school, you don't have to be a jerk to be popular!

"So, what sports do you play?" Jayla asks me.

"Um . . . I was thinking of trying soccer." Saying it out loud makes me feel more confident about the idea. It looks like the other kids are waiting for me to say more, so I blurt out, "And my sister plays field hockey." As if that has anything to do with me.

"Oh, right," Parker says. He turns to the others. "Her sister's Maisie Cooper."

Of course they instantly recognize her name. My sister leaves an impression everywhere she goes— apparently even in schools where she's never set foot.

"Is that why you were at that party at Owen's house?" Ashleigh asks.

I nod. "My sister's friends with his older brother."

"I still can't believe you went to that, Parker," Ashleigh says. "I mean, Owen Campbell? Really?"

Parker shrugs. "He used to be okay, back when we were kids."

"Yeah, but now he's so—"

PLOP!

Something lands in the middle of the table. It's a carton of milk, and it starts spraying everywhere, like a dairy sprinkler.

We all shriek and jump up, snatching up our food before it gets soaked with milk. Laughter explodes all around us as kids at the other tables realize what's happening.

"Who did that?" I ask, looking around. But no one answers me.

Instead, Ashleigh runs off to grab napkins and passes them out to everyone. I think of the way Courtenay's minions were falling all over themselves to clean up the milkshake she dropped. Shouldn't the other kids be rushing over to help? But no one does, so we get to work cleaning up the table ourselves.

As we finish sopping up the mess, a teacher finally comes by. "Everything okay over here?" he asks.

"Yup," Ashleigh says. "Just a spill."

The teacher clearly doesn't believe her, but he only nods and walks away.

"Why didn't you tell him what really happened?" I ask.

"We tried telling a teacher the first time," Parker explains, "when a pudding cup exploded under our table last year. It didn't help."

"They never figured out who did it, and the teachers started acting like *we* were the troublemakers," Ashleigh explains.

"Now we just ignore it," Hector adds.

"It's not worth it," Jayla says.

From the way they're talking, it sounds like this kind of thing happens all the time. And strangely, the things they're saying are a lot like what I would always say to Kat after one of Queen Courtenay's torture sessions. *Why bother telling anyone if she won't get in trouble?*

But that doesn't make sense. I'm me. And these are

the popular people. How could someone harass them like this and get away with it?

When the bell rings for the end of lunch, I follow Ashleigh over to the row of recycling bins, hoping I can follow her lead.

"Dumb jocks," someone hisses as they pass us.

"Just ignore them," Ashleigh tells me. But her cheeks turn bright pink.

It takes me a second to understand what she means. Wait, was that comment directed at *us*?

Alarm bells start going off in my head. Because suddenly this situation is so familiar. *Too* familiar. This has pretty much been my life for as long as I can remember, ever since Queen Courtenay sashayed into it. Pranks and jokes and muttered comments.

"B-but you're not dumb," I blurt out.

"Those kids are just being jerks," Ashleigh says. "Everyone thinks we're stupid because we play sports."

"But why would they say stuff like that to you? I mean, you're popular!"

Ashleigh laughs. "Popular? I wish." She shakes her head. "We used to all be friends, you know, when we were little. But these days, the science club kids rule this school. The rest of us, we're . . . well, I guess we're losers."

I blink and blink, trying to process what she's saying. But I can't believe it. After all my research and planning, how could I get things so completely wrong?

Ashleigh explains it to me as we head to our lockers. At Lincoln, no one cares if you're rich or good-looking—they care if you're smart and driven and trying to make a difference in the world. That's why Ashleigh isn't the queen of this school, like I was imagining. *Priya* is!

"Her whole family is amazing," Ashleigh tells me. "Back when her brother was the science club president, they raised a ton of money to install solar panels by the football field."

"Wow, her brother ran the club too?"

"Yeah, but he started high school last year, so Priya took over. She got the administration to add a bunch of different types of recycling bins so that less stuff will get thrown away." Ashleigh shrugs. "I mean . . .

all I do is kick a soccer ball around. Of course everyone likes the science kids better!"

I guess I see what she's saying, but I'm still stunned.

"You and Parker are like straight out of a nineties movie, though! You're the good-looking ones who can play sports! Everyone should worship you and be afraid of you!"

Ashleigh gives me a sad smile. "Too bad life isn't like a movie."

I walk through the rest of the school day in a haze. My head is still spinning when I get home and yank out my too-tight ponytail. I sit down at my computer and open up my spreadsheet. Then I grab my notebook and flip through the pages of scribbles from today. But all the data I collected is useless now!

I put my head in my hands, trying to think.

A minute later, I get a message from Kat. *How did it go???*

I groan and decide to video chat with her, since typing it out would take way too long.

"Did your plan really work?" she asks when she

answers. She's sprawled on her bed, painting her nails hot pink. The bookshelf behind her is so stuffed with manga, graphic novels, and art books, it looks like it might burst.

"Um . . . not exactly," I say.

A good scientist isn't supposed to talk too much about their experiment when it's not finished yet, for fear of messing up the results. But what happened today makes no sense. I need help understanding it.

"At Lincoln, the science club kids are kind of in charge," I explain. Then I tell her all the stuff Ashleigh told me about the social hierarchy at the school. "Even the nonscience kids are against the jocks. Which makes no sense, since Ashleigh and her friends seem totally nice."

Kat's quiet for a minute as she touches up the polish on her pinkie. Then she asks, "So this is bad news?"

"What do you mean?"

"Well, you probably fit right in with the science nerds, right? So shouldn't this be good news for you?

It means you've found your people *and* you can be popular!"

She's right. This *should* be good news. If there's a group I obviously belong with, it's the kids from science club! I was so worried about my experiment going wrong that I didn't even think about what this could mean.

This is actually . . . awesome! If the nerdy kids are popular, if they're the ones who never get bullied, then all I have to do is fly my geek flag at my new school and be safe!

"I need to refocus my Five Factors!" I cry.

"What does that mean?" Kat asks, but I'm too busy reading through my spreadsheet again to answer her. She must realize that I'm in Experiment Mode because she finally says she'll talk to me later and ends the call. I realize after she's hung up that I didn't ask her about her first day back. I'll have to remember to send her a message later.

Okay, so I thought I could be Ashleigh's minion, but it turns out I need to focus on Priya and get into her social group instead. Which is perfect, since her social group is made up of kids from the club!

The only problem, of course, is that I kind of blew off Priya and Owen today. I'll need to find a way to make it up to them.

And . . . I'll need to ditch Ashleigh and Parker. Obviously they're getting bullied, and I can't open myself up to that. When that milk carton hit the table at lunch today, for a second it was like I was back at the dance last year, my dress around my ankles and the entire school laughing at me. I can't go through that kind of humiliation again. I can't. If that means giving Ashleigh and Parker the cold shoulder, so be it.

I mean, who was I kidding anyway? Parker might not be the king of the school, but he's still not someone who'd ever be interested in me. And Ashleigh is nice enough, but pretty soon she'd have realized we have nothing in common. As for soccer . . . maybe I can join the team next year, after my social standing is solidified and I don't have to worry anymore.

As I start typing new goals into my spreadsheet, I ignore the uneasy feeling in my gut. The jocks were never going to be my real social group, after all. It was just for the experiment and protection. And now protecting myself means getting to be with my people. There's no point in feeling bad about it when it's the only logical step.

CHAPTER 7

The next morning, I wake up when it's still dark out to sneak in a little chemistry experiment before school. Exploding Emma posted a fun video last night that I have to try, especially since—unlike most of her experiments—this one is safe to do inside.

I play around with the fluid that I extracted from some glow sticks and see if I can make it glow brighter by mixing in dish soap. The result is awesome. I feel like a mad scientist creating a radioactive weapon or something.

As I'm finishing up, Dad comes shuffling into the kitchen. "A true scientist never sleeps, I see."

"What are you doing up so early?" I ask. Then I notice he's in workout clothes again. "Another hard-core training session with Uncle Joe?"

Dad lets out a tired laugh. "He said it'll be an easy one this time. No uphill sprints." He peers into the cups of glow stick liquid. "Wow, this is really something."

"I know. Adding that soap makes it look so much cooler."

Dad grins. "Hey, we didn't really get to talk about how your first day went."

"Well," I say slowly, "it wasn't exactly how I predicted it would be. But I think I'm going to get the hang of it."

"Good," Dad says. "I'm hoping I'll get the hang of this working-out thing too."

"You've never really been into it before," I point out. "Why now?"

Dad takes a sip of water. "I guess sometimes I look at what other people have, and it makes me wonder what else I could be doing with my life, you know? Of course I love my job, and I love you guys, but . . . I guess I've been looking for something more."

I can see how Uncle Joe's fancy job and apartment and car would make people jealous. But I never thought

Dad was into that kind of stuff. The thought of him in a convertible is pretty ridiculous.

Dad's phone buzzes. "Oh, Joe's here. I'll be back in a bit." Then he grabs a water bottle and heads out the door.

"Have fun!" I call, hoping my uncle really does go easy on him this time. Dad could hardly walk up and down the stairs after their last run.

I'm almost done cleaning up my experiment when Maisie comes rushing into the kitchen.

"You're not dressed yet?" she asks. She's already in her brand-new St. Mary's uniform, which would look a little fussy if she hadn't also dusted her hair and face with glitter.

Whoa. How did it get so late? I think this might be the first time Maisie's been ready for school before I am.

I quickly put the rest of my experiment away and run upstairs. When I throw open my closet, I'm suddenly frozen thinking about the Appearance Factor again. I've never stressed about what to wear before this year, unless it had to do with lab safety. Since I'm back to being my nerdy self today, I should put on one of my regular outfits. But the longer I stare at my wardrobe, the more I start to doubt that my regular stuff is nerdy enough for Priya and the other science kids. I need to take it up a notch.

Finally I decide on my favorite pair of jeans and the "Future Scientist" T-shirt that Dad got me for Christmas last year, which I've only ever dared to wear inside the house. I haven't even brushed my hair, but when I glance at the clock, I realize I'll miss the bus if I don't leave now. I'll have to wrangle my wavy mop into a ponytail on the ride to school.

Mom does a double take when I rush back down into the kitchen to grab a banana for the road. "You look . . . different, Blake," Mom says. "Is it still Blake?"

"Yup!" After introducing myself to everyone as Blake yesterday—and asking all my teachers to call me by my middle name—I can't suddenly change back to Lily, can I?

"Come on, Maisie," Mom says. "We need to get going."

St. Mary's is a few towns over, so Mom's going to

have to go out of her way to bring Maisie to school every day on her way to work. And then Dad will have to drive out there to pick her up in the afternoons. It seems weird that Maisie wouldn't just go to nearby Douglas High like a lot of her friends from Hemlock, but if my parents don't mind chaffeuring her around, then I guess it's fine.

Maisie grabs her backpack and gives me a hug goodbye.

"Good luck on your first day," I tell her, although I'm sure she doesn't need it.

"Thanks." She actually sounds a tiny bit nervous. Maybe even social chameleons stress out about starting at a new school? She gives me a wave and follows Mom out the door.

When they're gone, I finish stuffing my lunch into my bag and rush outside. I'm so late that at least it should be easy to avoid Parker and Ashleigh at the bus stop.

But no such luck. When I get on the bus, ready to slide into the first row of seats and hide my face, I hear Ashleigh calling out to me. "Blake, over here! I saved you a seat!"

I have no choice but to go over and sit down next to her. Then I glance back, wondering if any science club kids are here. The less they see me hanging out with the jocks, the better. Just in case, I slump lower in the seat.

"Hey, are those new?" Ashleigh asks, pointing to my hair.

"Huh?" I reach up—and realize that my safety glasses are still on my head!

I'm about to rip them off and stuff them in my bag when Ashleigh adds, "They're like a headband. So cute!"

Hmm. In that case, maybe I'll keep them on. At least they're keeping my untamed hair out of my face.

"So soccer starts next week. You're signing up, right?" Ashleigh asks after a minute.

"Oh, um. I don't know. I was thinking of doing something else this fall."

"Like what?"

I have to just tell her and get it over with. She'll figure it out soon enough anyway. "Um . . . like science club?"

Ashleigh's smile fades. "Oh."

"I just . . . I'm super into chemistry, you know? I love mixing things together and seeing what happens and doing experiments. And my old school didn't have a science club, so this is perfect for me." I realize I'm babbling. "I think I might fit in better there, that's all."

Ashleigh nods. "I get it. And we can still be friends, even if we're not on the soccer team together."

I swallow, suddenly feeling terrible. Here I am, ready to ditch Ashleigh, and she thinks we're already friends? I've never made friends with anyone so easily in my entire life! And I *was* looking forward to trying soccer again without Queen Courtenay there to turn it into a nightmare. Maybe my experiment doesn't need to include dumping Ashleigh completely.

"I mean, if soccer and the science club are on different days . . ." I say slowly.

Ashleigh lets out an excited squeal. "They are! Science club is on Mondays, and soccer is on Wednesdays and Fridays."

"Okay, well then . . ." I take a deep breath,

remembering the Attitude part of my Five Factors. Being popular means you act like you own the place and feel at ease no matter what. I might not be anywhere near feeling that way, but for now, I can fake it. "In that case, I'll do both."

All morning at school, I keep an eye out for Priya. I do spot her a few times, but she's always in a crowd. Now that I know she's really the queen of the seventh grade, I feel silly for not having realized it sooner. It's pretty obvious that she runs the show. She's always surrounded by an entourage: Owen—is he her boyfriend?—and at least a couple of her friends I've already started thinking of as Thing One and Thing Two. Hopefully she has room for a Thing Three.

After English, I finally spot Priya alone. Before I chicken out, I hurry over and comment on her earrings again. This time they're shaped like atoms.

"Those are even better than the double helixes," I tell her.

I see her taking in my T-shirt and my safety glasses. "Kind of a rebrand for you, huh?" she says.

"Um, what?" I ask, pretending I don't know exactly what she means.

She shrugs. "Whatever. You do you." Then she considers me for another second and adds, "I do like the safety glasses. It's a good look."

"Thanks," I say, adjusting them self-consciously.

Priya starts to head out of class, and I tag after her like a puppy. Now that she's talking to me, I'm not going to let her get away. "So when does the science club have its first meeting?" I ask, even though I already know the answer.

"Monday," she says. "There are signs about it everywhere."

"Oh, cool. Yeah. I think I saw those."

"Are you going to be there?" she asks.

"Yup! I'm like a total science geek. My old school didn't have a club, though. So this is awesome."

Priya stops walking and looks at me again. "So what's your cause?"

"M-my cause?"

"You know, like climate change or renewable energy or access to clean water."

I blink at her. "Well, obviously those are all good causes!"

She raises an eyebrow. "But if you had to pick one . . ."

"*Do* I have to pick one?"

"Yes," Priya says. "That's part of being in the club. We don't just do science for fun. We do it for the *world*. For example, I'm working on ways to reduce the school's carbon footprint, and Owen's focusing on the habitats of endangered animals."

"Wow." By comparison, my glow stick experiment from this morning seems pathetic.

She nods. "Yeah, so it's not enough to like chemistry or whatever. You need to *do* something with it. Otherwise, what's the point?"

Because it's fun? But that definitely seems like the wrong thing to say when I'm trying to get on her good side. Besides, maybe she's right. Maybe there is more that I could be doing than mixing various goopy substances in my kitchen.

"I'll think about it and come up with something by the first meeting," I tell her.

"Good. We don't have a lot of time to plan for the Science Showcase," she says. "And everyone in the club enters. It's required."

"Oh, okay." That *should* sound fun. I've always loved science fairs. But the way Priya's talking about it makes me kind of nervous.

She starts to walk away. Then she pauses and says, "Other kids have tried to join the club because they wanted to be part of our group, you know. But you can't fake it with us, Blake. You have to really mean it. Got it?"

I swallow, suddenly feeling as though Priya can see right through me. But I'm not faking it. I really do love science! And yes, maybe I have an ulterior motive for wanting to be in the club, but that doesn't change the fact that I'm a science geek through and through.

"Got it," I say.

She gives me another long look, as if she's trying to decide whether or not I've passed the test. Then she starts walking again. After a few steps, she glances over her shoulder. "Are you coming or not?"

"Coming where?" I ask.

"To lunch," she says. "You are sitting with us today, right? You don't have *someone else* to sit with?"

It's obvious she means Ashleigh and Parker. I guess I must have passed her test. And I'm definitely not going to blow my shot this time.

"Yeah! Yes! I'm coming!" I hurry after her before she can change her mind.

When we get to the cafeteria, I make it a point not to look toward Ashleigh's table. I don't need to feel guilty. I barely know her. And I have to do this for my experiment. But that doesn't mean I want to see the look of disappointment when she realizes I've switched sides.

When I sit down next to Priya, Owen grins at me from across the table. "Lil' Blake," he says. "So glad you could join us."

CHAPTER 8

When it comes to traditions, my family only has one: takeout and movie night every Friday. It's been our thing ever since I can remember.

Tonight, since it's the end of our first week of school, Maisie and I get to pick what type of food we want. We go with Italian since there's nothing better than stuffing yourself full of pasta and sauce and cheese.

"How's the half marathon training going, Dad?" Maisie asks over her lasagna.

He laughs. "Well, my body is more sore than it's ever been. But Joe says that's normal."

"Do you have a workout regimen so you can scale up your workouts over the next few weeks without overexerting yourself?" I ask.

"You've been doing some research, I see," Dad says. And of course, he's right. "Don't worry. Joe's handling the logistics. He says I'll definitely be ready in time."

Mom sighs. "Hon, you don't need to keep impressing my brother. He won't think any less of you if you say no."

"I'm not doing this to impress anyone," Dad says. "What's so bad about wanting to get in shape? And you said it yourself, it's for a good cause."

I can tell Mom wants to push, but maybe she doesn't think it's worth it. Whatever weird power my uncle has over my dad, Mom has never been able to stop it before.

Instead, she turns to me and asks, "How's school going now that you're the new, improved you, Lily? I mean Blake?"

"Good," I say. "Better than good, actually. Pretty great." I tell my family about the science club meeting on Monday and about the showcase. "I need to come up with a really amazing project."

"I'm sure you will," Dad tells me. "You're a smart kid."

"And I might join the soccer team," I add.

Mom's eyebrows shoot up. "That's great! You used to love playing when you were little. I never really understood why you quit. And it's good for you to branch out and try different things."

My excitement dims. Because I know she really means "things other than weird science experiments."

Luckily Dad jumps in before Mom can say anything else to make me feel bad. "How is school going for *you* so far, Mais?"

I expect my sister to chime in with "Great!" because that's usually her response to everything. But instead, she shrugs and says, "Okay. They made me wipe off my eye shadow today. 'No glitter allowed.'"

"How are you going to survive?" I say, laughing.

I'm surprised when no one else joins in. Maisie and I joke about her glitter obsession all the time. But apparently this time it's not funny.

"You'll figure it out, Mais," Mom says, which doesn't really make sense.

"Figure what out?" I ask.

Maisie only shakes her head and gives me a bright

smile. "Nothing. It's fine." Then she starts chattering on about her classes and some kids she met and how much she already loves her French teacher.

But I can't stop thinking about that smile and how fake it looked.

When I go shopping with Kat the next day, I remember all over again how much I've missed seeing her at school. As we wander through the outdoor mall—which is actually a comfortable temperature, for once—Kat tells me about everything I'm missing out on this year.

"Our English teacher is so evil. She already assigned like three essays. But the art teacher is amazing. He's having us all enter a contest in a couple of weeks. The winners get their pieces featured in an art show at a real gallery in town."

"Wow! That's perfect for you."

"Only if my stuff gets picked," she says. "I'll have to really work to make it good enough. The teacher said the contest winners in the past have mostly been eighth graders."

"You'll get accepted for sure," I tell her. It's funny that Kat is so confident about everything else in her life, but when it comes to art, she's actually pretty insecure. I guess because it means so much to her.

We don't have much luck shopping, so we take a break and swing by a burger place for a snack.

When we sit down with a heaping plate of french fries, Kat opens up her bag and pulls out her own bottle of ketchup.

"I still can't believe you carry that thing around!" I say with a laugh.

She shrugs. "The stuff in packets doesn't taste the same," she says. "If you ever tried it, you'd see."

"No way. Ketchup isn't even food."

She only smiles and douses her half of the fries. "So what's this science club like anyway?" she asks.

"It's great!" I tell her about Priya and all the things she and her brother have done to improve the school.

"Wow, she sounds really intense," Kat says.

"She is, but it's kind of awesome. She and her friends are actually making a difference in the world."

Kat crinkles her nose. "Not everything has to be

for a cause. I mean, my comics are just for fun. Is that really so bad?"

"No, but what if they could be more?" I ask. "Wouldn't you want to give it a shot?"

"I guess," Kat says with a shrug. "But we're in middle school. How are we supposed to know what our big cause is?"

This might be one of those things we need to agree to disagree on, like our years-old debate on whether science is better than art. So I change the topic. "Anyway, it's funny how everyone worships the science club kids. Even the teachers let them get away with whatever they want," I say, remembering how easily Priya got a hall pass from the main office that first day. And Owen told me that sometimes the science teachers won't give the club kids homework so they can spend more time on their projects.

"Wow," Kat says. "That is nuts."

"It's so great, Kat. I can totally embrace my geek self and be accepted! My experiment is working perfectly."

"Lucky. With you gone, Queen Courtenay's been focusing all her energy on me."

"Ugh, I'm sorry."

"Oh, don't worry," Kat assures me. "I'm not letting her get to me."

But there's no way that's true. I don't care how strong Kat is—or pretends to be. That kind of torture wears on you after a while.

"Did I tell you my dad's doing a half marathon with my uncle?" I ask, hoping to cheer her up.

Kat groans. "No way!" She loves hearing about all the weird stuff Dad does to impress Mom's brother.

"Yup. Uncle Joe talked him into attaching weights to his ankles when he went for a run this morning. He came back so exhausted, he could barely lift his legs. He went to stretch on the living room floor and wound up falling asleep on the carpet. Mom vacuumed around him like he was a piece of furniture!"

Now we're both giggling. Maybe it's a little mean to make fun of my dad, but he did look really funny sleeping on the floor.

We finish up our fries and go back to shopping, combing through the sales racks at a couple of clothing stores.

"So, is your neighbor in the science club too?" Kat asks as she looks through some jeans.

"My neighbor?"

"Come on, Lily. You know I mean Parker Tanaka!"

"Actually, no. He's not. It turns out the science club kids think he's a dumb jock. That would probably make him the king at any other middle school, but at Lincoln, he's kind of an outcast."

"Wow," Kat says. "He's so cute, though."

"I know! And really nice too."

She raises an eyebrow. "Does that mean you've actually talked to him since the pool party?"

"Kind of. But I guess it doesn't matter since he's not popular."

Kat looks at me like I've suddenly sprouted another head. "Why not?"

"Because having a crush on him doesn't fit into my experiment." Boyfriend/Guy Friend obviously only applies to boys who are popular too.

"Wait," Kat says. "Why do you even *have* to finish your experiment? You're already in with the popular crowd, aren't you?"

"Not really. They're letting me sit with them at lunch, but I have to prove myself to them. I'm not safe yet. If I don't come up with a really good showcase project—"

"They'll kick you out?" Kat asks in disbelief. "Do you even want to be part of a group that would do that to you?"

"It's better than being part of a group that gets milk-bombed during lunch," I say. "Besides, like you said, the science kids are my people. It makes sense for me to be with them."

"If they're 'your people,' then why do you have to prove yourself? Shouldn't they just accept you?"

I roll my eyes. "That's not how it works. It's all part of my research. They need to know I'm one of them, that's all."

But I can tell Kat's not convinced.

CHAPTER 9

When the first science club meeting comes around on Monday afternoon, I'm totally nervous. I have an idea for what I want my focus to be, but I'm afraid it won't be good enough.

"It's no secret we have the most fun in this club," Miss Turner, the club advisor, says with a chuckle. "We work hard and we play hard. No one knows more about that than our president, Priya Joshi, and vice president, Owen Campbell."

Everyone claps and cheers as the two of them step forward. Considering that some of the kids are clearly in eighth grade, it's pretty impressive that they're so excited about a couple of seventh graders being in charge.

"Back when Priya's brother was our president," Miss Turner goes on, "he really put this club on the map. We were new and unknown, with only a handful of members. But thanks to Ravi's drive and vision, we were able to make a huge impact on this school, and now look at us!" She gestures around the jam-packed room. There must be at least thirty of us here.

I glance at Priya and am surprised to see a hard look on her face. You'd think with everyone praising her brother, she'd be beaming with pride.

Miss Turner turns to Priya. "Would you like to say a few words?"

She shrugs. "Sure. Last year, we made the club's mission to have better recycling options brought into the school. This year, we're focusing on ways to decrease Lincoln's carbon footprint."

"I'll be setting up a meeting with the principal soon so that Owen and Priya can share some of their ideas," Miss Turner chimes in, adjusting her purple glasses.

I'm not the only person in the room with my mouth hanging open. I've never been around kids my age who sound so driven and focused and mature. It's almost like they're grown-ups. No wonder everyone worships them!

"As you probably know," Priya goes on, "the Science Showcase is held in late October."

"Anyone can enter the showcase, but we pretty much expect the top three winners to be from the science club," Owen says.

"Priya's and Owen's projects tied for first place last year," Miss Turner adds.

"What's the prize?" a boy asks. "Cash?"

"No," Miss Turner admits. "But you get something even better."

"They send the top three winners to the annual youth science fair in Boston after the New Year," Priya says.

Owen's eyes shine with excitement. "It's totally platinum. There are all these celebrity scientists that you get to meet."

"There are goofy YouTubers like Exploding Emma too," Priya breaks in, "but then there are people who do *real* science. Life-changing stuff."

I barely hear what else they say because my brain is stuck on Exploding Emma. Oh my goodness. Now I *really* have to place in the top three—I might get to meet her in person!

"That's why this club isn't a regular club," Priya goes on. "It's pretty much our lives. We meet every week and sometimes on weekends. This club has to be your top priority or you don't belong here. So if you're not ready to make that kind of commitment, now's the time to let us know." She points toward the door and waits.

For a second nobody moves, as if they're trying to figure out whether she's joking. I expect Miss Turner to remind Priya that the club is for everyone, but she only watches silently. I guess she was serious about the whole "work hard, play hard" thing.

Finally the boy who asked about the prize shrugs and walks toward the door. "Sorry," he says before hurrying out. A couple of other kids follow him, but everyone else stays put.

To be honest, I'm pretty intimidated by the whole thing. But also excited. This is my chance to finally throw myself into science and be around people who are as dedicated as I am.

"Okay, good," Priya says. "Then let's get into small groups and talk about ideas for our projects."

I wind up in a group with Priya, Owen, and the girl with her hair in tiny braids who I've been calling Thing Two—her name turns out to be Bree. Priya describes her plan to decrease Lincoln's carbon footprint by 30 percent in the next two years. Then Owen talks about how he wants to expand his database of endangered species to include data from around the whole state.

"If I graph it out for everyone," he says, "they'll see how declining habitats are affecting different species."

"Wow," Bree says. "That's cool."

"And I was thinking of using some of my photographs too," Owen goes on. "So they can put a face on the data."

But Priya shakes her head. "The numbers are the important part," she says. "If you put a bunch of pictures in, no one will take it seriously."

I don't really agree with that, but Priya seems so certain that I don't say anything.

"You're right," Owen says automatically, and I

have the feeling he'd agree with Priya no matter what she said.

Then Bree talks about making an app that tracks the common cold as it spreads through specific schools. "If you get sick, you mark it in the app, and then it can predict which schools will be hit the hardest and when."

My idea seems so silly in comparison. I don't have any hard data or an app. But when Owen turns to me, I have no choice but to share.

"Well, my project would have to do with bullying."

Priya raises an eyebrow. "Okay . . ."

"I want to come up with a formula that will keep kids from being bullied. Basically, give them criteria that will help them fit in at their school so that they can fly under the radar and be left alone by the bullies."

"That sounds interesting," Bree says, giving me an encouraging smile.

But Priya doesn't seem convinced. "Where would you get these criteria?"

"Um, from research," I say. "You know, TV and movie trends and, um, social media and stuff." I don't want to admit that I've already done a bunch of the research and it led me in the wrong direction. But I still think I'm onto something. If I'd had my Five Factors when I'd first started at Hemlock, maybe I could have avoided years of bullying. And there has to be a way to make it work for any school, where you plug in different variables depending on the social scene there.

"It sounds pretty vague," Owen points out.

"Yeah, I'm still working on it." I'm not ready to share my Five Factors of Popularity yet, even though I'm pretty sure I'm on the right track. It feels too risky considering my experiment is still in its early stages.

"And the idea sounds kind of soft," Priya says. "More like sociology than like real science."

"Sociology is real science," I say. "It's the science of behavior."

Owen shakes his head. "The way people act is so open to interpretation. It's not like data you can really crunch."

I want to point out how untrue that is. Sociology has plenty of hard data. But it's obvious Priya and

Owen don't see it that way, and the last thing I want to do is get on their bad sides after I just managed to eke out an invitation to be in their group. I glance over at Bree, but she's flipping through her notebook, clearly staying out of the debate.

"What if you did bullying statistics instead?" Priya says. "You know, show people the numbers to get their attention."

Honestly, that sounds really boring. But Priya was one of the winners of the showcase last year. She must know what she's talking about.

"Yeah, maybe."

"You need something with a measurable impact, you know?" she adds. "Something real."

I don't know why she thinks an anti-bullying formula wouldn't have a real impact. Clearly *she's* never been humiliated in front of her entire school.

CHAPTER 10

The rest of the week goes by in a blur. I video chat with Kat for about five minutes on Wednesday night—she's so busy working on her entry for the art exhibit that I don't even have time to ask her advice on my showcase project.

In the mornings, I sit on the bus with Ashleigh, keeping an eye out for anyone from science club. Parker sits behind us and chimes in occasionally. I still can't really look at him without my face growing boiling hot, but he doesn't seem to notice.

And at lunch, I sit with Priya and Owen and the rest of their group: Bree, whose common cold app is coming along great; Francesca (aka Thing One), who's researching ways to use cloning in food production;

and a quiet boy named Ryder, whose showcase project is about possible medical uses for algae. It's awesome how they talk about new scientific breakthroughs and fun experiments people want to try and great books and shows they've been into lately. It feels amazing to be around kids who really get how incredible science can be.

"I saw this hilarious video," I announce one day, eager to contribute to the conversation. "This girl made her own invisible ink and then had it explode all over a wall." I don't mention that it was an Exploding Emma video, remembering that Priya isn't exactly a fan.

Bree chuckles, at least, but Priya rolls her eyes and says, "I don't know why people waste their time on junk science when there's real research they could be doing."

Owen doesn't even look up from typing something on his phone.

Oops. After that, I make sure to only talk about things that sound like "real science." Whatever that means.

By the end of the week, I notice other people are starting to treat me differently. The teachers are calling on me more and the other kids are looking at me with respect. Every once in a while, someone will compliment me on my safety glasses, which I've been wearing in my hair every day. They're starting to feel like my trademark.

At my old school, I'd rush through the halls keeping my head down, hoping no one would notice me. Here, I find myself walking more slowly, keeping my head up, making eye contact, even smiling at people. Is this what being popular feels like? If so, it's incredible.

I only wish Kat were here with me to enjoy it. The science club kids are cool, but none of them have her sense of humor. And I've heard great things about the art club at Lincoln, which I'm sure she'd love.

After the last bell on Friday, Ashleigh rushes over to my locker. "So, are you coming to soccer?"

I've been debating all day. I did bring my gym clothes, just in case, but am I really going to go through with it? If anyone from the club sees me . . . And yet, this is my chance to give soccer another shot, on my terms instead of Queen Courtenay's. And isn't this part of Factor 3: Social Life? Joining clubs and activities and actually enjoying them? Maisie has always juggled multiple clubs and sports without a problem. Why can't I?

"Yes," I tell Ashleigh. "I'm in."

I follow her down to the locker room to get changed, and then we head out to the field. There are only about a dozen kids here, and Ashleigh tells me that half of them are new this year.

"We're not exactly a popular sport," she admits. "Last season, we had to forfeit a couple of games because we didn't have enough players."

When Parker sees me, he gives me a high five and says, "You made it!"

My hand tingles from where it touched his. "I'm glad I came," I tell him, and it's true.

We start by practicing dribbling and simple footwork. After stretches and a water break, Coach has us do some shooting drills before we break into two teams for a scrimmage. It's been years since I've played, and

I trip over my own feet more than I'd like, but the other kids on my team don't yell at me the way they would at my old school. Everyone just cheers me on and tells me to keep trying. I forgot how fun it is to kick the ball around and tear across the field. It almost feels like I'm in kindergarten again, playing for the first time and loving every minute of it.

"Welcome to the team, everyone!" Coach Nazari says as we cool down at the end of practice. "I believe each team member should have a chance to play, no matter their skill level. But we'll be doing a lot of work these next few weeks to get us ready for our first game!"

I can't believe it. I'm going to be playing in a real soccer game! Mom is going to freak out when I tell her.

By the time I get home, I'm sweaty and exhausted but in a good mood. I find Dad slumped over the kitchen table, also clearly sweaty and exhausted.

"Are you okay?" I ask him when he barely moves at the sight of me.

"I think all this training is going to kill me," he says with a weak laugh.

"Can't you give your half marathon spot to someone

else?" I say. "Try again next year when you've had more time to train?"

"Your uncle's depending on me. Plus, it's a fundraiser. People have already pledged money."

"But—"

"Besides, it's good to have a healthy goal. Makes you push yourself."

I guess that's true. If only he didn't look so miserable.

"How's school going?" he asks. "Haven't seen you around much."

"It's good. I was actually at soccer practice. Our first game is in a few weeks!"

"Wow, congrats, kiddo!" Dad says. "That's awesome."

Just then Maisie comes in carrying a stack of textbooks.

"What's awesome?" she asks.

"Blake joined the soccer team."

"Wow!" she says. "Good for you."

"What about you, Mais?" Dad asks. "I haven't heard anything about field hockey. When are tryouts?"

"Oh. I decided not to do it this year."

My jaw drops. "What? But you love field hockey."

She shrugs. "It takes up too much of my time. And I don't know anyone on the St. Mary's team."

Huh. Since when has not knowing people stopped my sister from doing anything?

I want to press, but Dad jumps in with "Well, if that's what you want to do, Mais, it's your decision." He glances at the clock. "So it looks like it's going to be just us for our Friday takeout and movie. Mom has to work late. Any requests? I thought we could get pizza and watch that new Pixar movie."

"Actually, I was invited to a study group tonight," Maisie says.

Dad and I both stare at her.

"You're studying on a Friday night?" I ask.

She shrugs again. "There weren't any parties going on, so I figured it's better than nothing."

"What about you, Blake?" Dad asks.

"I should work on ideas for the Science Showcase project."

"Okay, no worries. We can do it tomorrow night

instead," Dad says. "I'm glad things are going well for both my girls at your new schools, but don't forget that we like having you around too, okay?"

Maisie laughs while I roll my eyes. But I can't help smiling. "Okay, Dad," I say.

CHAPTER 11

On Monday, I come to school armed with new ideas for my showcase project. The plan is to run them by Owen at lunch before Priya hears them at the club meeting later. That way I can weed out the ones he doesn't think are good. I like Priya—or, at least, I admire her—but I'm also kind of scared of her. I definitely want to impress her.

But when I get to lunch, Owen's seat is empty.

When I ask Bree if she's seen him, she shrugs and says, "I think he's meeting with Miss Turner about something."

"Oh," I say, unable to hide my disappointment.

Priya surprises me by leaning over and whispering, "You like him, don't you?"

"Wh-what? Who?" Is she talking about Parker? But how could she know about that?

"Come on, Blake," she says. "I saw the way you guys were around each other at the pool party. It was pretty obvious. That's really why you wanted to join the science club, isn't it?"

I blink, finally understanding who she's talking about. "Wait, Owen? You think I like Owen?"

"Why not? You two would be cute together," Priya says.

"*So* cute," Bree chimes in. I guess she's been listening to our whole conversation. Luckily Francesca and Ryder are on the other side of the table and not paying attention to us.

"You guys have so much in common," Priya goes on. "I mean, it only makes sense."

I blink at her. "But I thought you and Owen . . ." The way he hangs on her every word, it really seems like he likes her. Plus, I assumed that Priya would be dating someone.

Priya shakes her head. "He used to have a little thing for me, but we're just friends. No, I think you should go for it."

It probably is time I started working on the Boyfriend/Guy Friend part of my plan. But Owen? I've never thought of him that way. Although I guess on paper we make a lot more sense than Parker and I do.

"But I don't even know if Owen thinks of me that way," I say.

"Don't worry. I'll find out if he likes you," Priya tells me.

"What? How?"

Priya shrugs. "Simple. I'll ask him."

Before I can object, a chorus of shouts rings out on the other side of the cafeteria. Everyone turns toward the sound, which is coming from Ashleigh and Parker's table.

Uh-oh. Another exploding milk carton?

But no, it's worse this time. It looks like an entire plate of spaghetti erupted all over the table. I can see chunks of tomato sauce in Ashleigh's hair. She and her friends are rushing around, already cleaning up the mess. It looks like Jayla's on the verge of tears.

It kills me to sit there and watch the humiliation,

but what can I do? So I turn away, my stomach churning.

"I don't get it," I say, half to myself. "Who would do that?"

"Owen told me it's probably the remedials," Bree says.

"The who?"

Bree points to a group I've never seen before, sitting a few tables over. "The people who take all the lower classes, you know, for the not-so-smart kids," she explains. "They're always getting into trouble. Last year, one of them threw a chair out the window and got expelled."

I study the kids she's talking about. They're laughing loudly at the prank, but they're not acting particularly guilty. I don't know why they'd target Ashleigh and Parker. Then again, I don't know why anyone would.

That night, I get a video call from Kat. Her face is glowing with excitement. "I did it!" she says. "One of my drawings got picked for the fall art exhibit!"

"Whoa, that's awesome! I knew you'd get in."

"I was the only seventh grader picked," she says. "Queen Courtenay made all these comments about how only losers do the art show, but that's because her stuff isn't going to hang in a real gallery!"

"I didn't know she was into art."

"She's not, but everyone in our class entered a piece. She's annoyed that mine got picked and hers didn't. I heard her dad giving her a hard time about it after school, about her 'not excelling' and all that. You know how he is."

My excitement dims. I do know how Assistant Dean Lyons is. He's not cruel like Courtenay, but he's pretty obsessed with keeping up appearances. That's why he'd never admit that his daughter tortures other kids, but he also won't let her get away with being less than perfect at anything.

"Be careful, okay? You know what she's like when she's mad."

Kat rolls her eyes. "Oh, please. I can handle it. What is she going to do to me?"

But that's the thing. With Courtenay, you never know. I guess that's part of being the queen bee. You can lash out and sting whoever you want, whenever you feel like it. There don't seem to be any rules. Thank goodness Priya isn't like that.

"How was your science club meeting?" Kat asks, settling back on her bed.

"Oh, um. Fine, I guess."

"Whoa, that is not the reaction I was expecting. I thought that club was your life."

"It is. It's just . . ." I sigh. "Priya hated my showcase ideas. I tried every approach to my bullying formula that I could think of, but she said she doesn't think the topic 'has legs.' She wants me to come up with something else."

"That's ridiculous," Kat says, shaking her head. "You're already doing the experiment. You have a bunch of data. You should do something with it."

"My project needs to be in the top three," I say. "If Priya doesn't think my topic is good enough, then I'll have to come up with something better."

"What about doing one of those Exploding Emma things?" Kat asks.

"You want me to make a volcano or something?"

I laugh. "Priya thinks those kinds of experiments are 'junk science.'"

"Who cares what she thinks?" Kat says.

I do, but that doesn't seem like the right answer. So instead I say, "She and Owen tied for first place last year. They know what they're talking about."

Besides, I'm sure I can come up with something better. A project that really means something. I just hope I can do it in time.

CHAPTER 12

Wednesday's soccer practice goes even better than the first one. I run around with a huge smile on my face the entire time. I can't believe how great it feels to be back out on the field, to be a part of a team. And it doesn't hurt that I get to spend more time with Parker, either.

The next morning, Owen is waiting for me at my locker. Huh. He's never done that before.

"Hey, Lil' Blake," he says when I go over to him. For some reason, he sounds nervous. But he seemed totally normal at lunch yesterday. "So listen, I talked to Priya last night and . . ."

My stomach lurches as I remember Priya saying that she'd find out if Owen liked me. Oh no. He must think I have a crush on him, and he's here to let me down gently.

"And I was wondering," he goes on. "What are you doing after school tomorrow?"

"T-tomorrow? Why?"

"Maybe you and I could hang out."

My jaw falls open. Owen wants to hang out with me after school, just the two of us? Maybe he really does like me!

"We could go out for ice cream or something," he adds.

"Like a date?" I blurt, thinking of the last time Maisie met a guy for ice cream.

Owen chuckles. "Yeah, sure. Whatever you want to call it."

Oh my gosh! A date! A real date!

"Um, yeah," I say, trying not to sound like I'm about to burst with excitement. "Yes, that sounds fun."

"Platinum," he says. "I'll meet you here after school."

He starts to turn away, but then I remember that tomorrow is Friday. That means I have soccer again.

The first two practices were so much fun that I was really looking forward to the next one.

"Wait," I call after Owen. "I forgot that I have . . ." I trail off, realizing I can't tell Owen the truth. The science club kids will never understand why I'm still hanging out with the jocks. And besides, this is my chance to tackle the Boyfriend/Guy Friend part of my plan.

"You have what?" Owen asks.

"Um, homework. I have homework to do."

"We can do it together," Owen says. "And we can talk about your showcase project. Priya says you still don't have a solid idea?"

I swallow. "I'm working on it."

"Don't worry. We'll come up with something good," he says, flashing me a bright smile. "So we're on for tomorrow?"

What can I do? I can't turn him down. He's the most popular boy in my grade. And I really do need his help with my project. I can miss one soccer practice, can't I? I bet no one will even notice.

"Okay," I tell him. "Let's do it."

I practically float through the rest of the day, in disbelief that I have my first actual date in just over twenty-four hours! Kat is going to die when I tell her.

But when I get to science class, I try to pull myself together. Miss Turner is tough on everyone, but I feel like I need to prove myself even more because I'm in science club.

As Bree and I team up to work on today's experiment—seeing if we can slow down the rate of a chemical reaction—I'm even more careful than I would be at home.

When I go back to triple-check the instructions, Bree leans over and whispers, "I think we're okay. We don't have to get it perfect."

But I can practically feel Miss Turner watching us from across the room. "Don't you think we have to get it right, though, since we're in the science club?"

"Maybe," Bree says. "But that doesn't mean we have to suck all the fun out of it."

I look at her in surprise. This is the first time I've really talked to Bree without Owen or Priya around. For all the notes I have on her in my spreadsheet, it dawns on me that I don't actually know her very well.

"I didn't realize we were allowed to have fun and do science at the same time," I half whisper.

She laughs. "I know Priya is pretty intense. But if you knew her brother, you'd totally understand."

"Ravi?" I ask. "Didn't he used to be the club president?"

She nods. "He pretty much ruled this school. He's like this little scrawny guy, but he's super driven. I bet he'll be a real scientist one day." She lowers her voice. "I think it's kind of rough on Priya."

"What do you mean?"

"Well, imagine if you had an older sibling who was basically perfect. Not exactly easy shoes to fill, you know?"

I don't have to imagine it. I live it every day. But at least Maisie and I have always been into different things—and now that I'm at Lincoln and she's at St. Mary's, our teachers aren't comparing us to each other. I guess I can see why Priya's so intense all the time. I'll have to add this to the notes I've been keeping on her.

"Ladies," Miss Turner says, walking by. "Less chatting, more experimenting, please."

My cheeks turn hot at getting in trouble, but when Bree flashes me a smile, I grin back at her.

CHAPTER 13

After school the next day, I hurry to my locker, my stomach fluttering as I go to meet Owen. When I asked Kat for advice, she told me "not to worry" and to "have fun," which wasn't exactly helpful. I guess she doesn't realize what a big deal this is—for me *and* for my experiment. So I also spent an hour last night researching date etiquette, wanting to make sure I get it right.

Maybe I shouldn't put so much pressure on my first date, but checking Guy Friend (or maybe even Boyfriend???) off my list would bring me a whole lot closer to the optimal result for my experiment.

I've worn my most science chic outfit to date: a pair of leggings with a microbe pattern on them, a "There

Is No Planet B" T-shirt, and my trusty lime-green safety glasses in my hair. Maisie helped me pick out the outfit online the other day, and Mom was actually happy to buy it since I'm finally taking an interest in my appearance.

When Owen comes over to my locker, he gives me a bright smile. "Awesome shirt," he says.

"Thanks. You look nice too." And he does. He's wearing a NASA cap that matches the color of his eyes and an unbuttoned flannel with a T-shirt underneath that says "Fe Man."

"Iron Man, I like it," I say.

"Thanks," he says. "Ready to go?"

I nod, suddenly too jittery to speak. Owen might not be quite as adorable as Parker, but he's still cute and super smart. Technically he's totally my type.

As we head down the hall, I can't believe that I'm walking with the most popular boy in my grade. Imagine if Queen Courtenay could see me now! Okay, she'd probably make fun of Owen for being a nerd. But once she figured out his social status, she'd be sucking up to him in no time. And the kids around us definitely notice. I even see one girl glaring at me. It probably sounds terrible to admit, but the look on her face fills me with glee. *I* am making someone else jealous!!

But as we head out of school, I realize we're going to walk right past the soccer field. Oh no. I didn't tell anyone that I wasn't going to be at soccer practice today, since I didn't want to lie and come up with an excuse. So they're probably expecting me.

I try to keep my head down and walk as fast as I can.

"Whoa, slow down, Lil' Blake!" Owen says. "What's the rush?"

"Oh, I'm just, um, really sensitive to the sun," I blurt out.

"Here." Owen pulls off his NASA hat and puts it on my head. "Better?"

"Thanks," I say, melting at the sweet gesture. But then I glance toward the soccer field, and I spot Ashleigh standing near the bleachers.

She's staring right at us, a look of confusion on her face that quickly turns to disappointment.

I duck my head down and keep walking. I feel bad about ditching practice. But my experiment is going so well. I can't give it up now!

When we get into town, Owen and I head to Three Scoops. I've only ever been here with Kat, and we usually come to gawk at boys, since there are none at Hemlock. Now I'm the one here with a boy!

We go up to order, and I open my mouth to ask for a dish of chocolate Oreo, but then Owen starts bombarding the guy behind the counter with a million questions about where the milk is from and if it's organic and how sustainable the cow farm is. It's all important stuff, I know. But my stomach is growling and I kind of just want some ice cream.

Finally Owen decides on some mango sorbet because it's vegan. I feel like such a planet-hating monster for wanting to order chocolate that I go for the sorbet too, even though mango always makes my tongue tingle a little.

We both pay for our own cups, which is fine. Expecting the boy to pay is so outdated. Still, I'm a little disappointed that he didn't at least offer. That's what a lot of my research said should happen, since he's the one who asked me out.

As we grab a table, I peek at the other people to see if they're looking at us. I'm so busy thinking about it that I don't even realize Owen and I are sitting in silence until I glance at him and see an expectant look on his face. Oh. I guess we should be trying to have a conversation.

"So, did you want to study?" I ask.

Owen shrugs. "Not really," he says. "I just wanted to hang out with you."

I feel my cheeks flush. Wow. I guess I *was* wrong about him having a crush on Priya.

"So, how are you liking Lincoln so far?" he asks.

"It's good," I say. "I definitely fit in a lot better here than at my old school. People there were so snotty. Everyone cared about what you looked like and how much money you had."

Owen groans. "That sounds like a nightmare."

"Yeah, it was." The more I talk, the less nervous I feel. "There were no kids like you and Priya, trying to do good stuff. I mean, we did a lot of fundraising, but it was always so the school could get even fancier. Last year, we had a silent auction so that we could build a second tennis court!"

"You'd think if they had that much money, they could do something worthwhile with it, like invest in a wind turbine."

"I know," I say. "But the worst thing was the popular group. They'd bully all the nerdy kids. I definitely don't miss that."

"That's rough." Owen peers out the window for a moment, as if he's deep in thought, and then he asks, "Did you know that Parker and I used to be friends, back in elementary school?"

I swallow a bite of sorbet, the mango making my tongue tingle as predicted. "I heard something about that. What happened?"

"He started doing sports and his new jock friends didn't like me. They'd throw rocks at me after school and stuff. He might seem like a nice guy now, but he wasn't always like that."

"Is that really true?" I can't imagine Parker throwing *rocks* at anyone.

Owen nods, and the pain in his face makes it clear that he's still not over it. Priya might not know what it feels like to be bullied, but Owen obviously does.

"So don't you think that's all the more reason I should do my anti-bullying formula for my project?" I ask. "It could really help people."

"Science is about results," Owen says, shaking his head. "If you have a problem, you use science to solve it. What you're talking about is changing people's behavior. That's not something you can measure. I don't think people *can* change their behavior. We are who we are."

I want to laugh. If only he could see what my life was like a few weeks ago, he'd see how measurable and changeable human behavior can be.

"But the good news is that you're at Lincoln now," he goes on. "And you're one of us. You don't have to worry anymore." He reaches out and puts his hand on mine. "How does that sound?"

Forget the tingling on my tongue. Suddenly my entire body is tingling. "That sounds perfect."

CHAPTER 14

We're in the middle of takeout-and-movie family night when the doorbell rings. I'm shocked to find Priya standing on my porch, looking even more serious than usual. We'd made plans for her to come by tonight so we could talk about our showcase projects, but she's almost two hours early!

"I thought we said seven thirty?" I say, still chewing a bite of pizza.

"Science club business can't wait," she insists.

"Um, okay."

Priya waves over her shoulder to a car parked in front of my house. Someone in the passenger seat waves back, and the car pulls away.

"Your parents?" I ask as we go inside.

She nods. "They're on their way to some awards ceremony for my brother," she says. "They'll come pick me up after."

Huh. I wonder if that's the real reason she's here. Maybe she didn't want to watch people fawning over her brother yet again. "What award?" I ask.

She shrugs. "It's like the third one this month. I can't keep track." Or maybe Priya *isn't* jealous of her brother—she seems totally indifferent. Then again, she's always so hard to read.

I lead her through the living room and tell my parents we'll be upstairs working.

Mom is clearly over the moon to see me hanging out with a friend on a Friday night, but Dad looks dejected. Probably because Maisie's off at her study group again, so family night is getting smaller by the minute.

"Are you sure you two don't want to watch with us for a little while first?" he asks. "There's plenty of pizza left."

"That's okay, Dad," I say. "But thanks."

In my room, I turn on some music to make things

feel a little less awkward. I'm used to having Kat over, but I can't remember the last time I hung out with anyone else in here. This is good, though. It aligns perfectly with my goals for Factor 3: Social Life.

Priya walks around, inspecting my books and posters. I'm surprised when I hear her singing along to one of the pop songs on my playlist. I figured she'd only be into classical music or something.

"You have a really good voice," I say.

She blinks at me, as if she didn't even realize that she was singing. Then she shrugs and mumbles, "Thanks."

My room must pass inspection because she finally sits on my bed and says, "So I heard you and Owen had a good time on your date. I knew I was right."

The truth is, I didn't have a crush on him before. But after hanging out with him this afternoon, well . . . I can see why Priya thought we'd be cute together.

"You really don't mind?" I ask.

She shakes her head. "Owen and I are better as friends. And he likes you. I can tell."

I feel myself blush. "I think I like him too," I say.

"Good." She reaches into her bag and pulls out a notebook. Suddenly she's all business. "Okay, Owen said you're still figuring out your project. We don't have a lot of time, Blake. If you're in the club, then your project has to be one of the best. Otherwise, you'll make us look bad."

I take a deep breath, deciding to give my idea one more shot. "I still think the anti-bullying formula could work. I've collected tons of data and—"

"Okay, let's see it."

"Wh-what?" I've never shown my raw data to anyone, not even Kat.

"Having lots of data isn't enough," Priya says. "It needs to be usable. Show me what you have and maybe we can work with it." Then, before I can stop her, she opens up my laptop.

"Wait!" I cry, but it's too late. My computer turns on, revealing my spreadsheet. I must have left it open.

I watch, frozen, as Priya starts to scroll through my notes. I've used initials and abbreviations instead of names and places, but will that be enough to keep her from realizing that it's all about her and the other kids at Lincoln?

Thankfully, she skims through it in about ten seconds and then turns back to me. "So you've boiled popularity down to five factors?" she asks, raising a skeptical eyebrow.

I nod, relieved that she hardly looked at what I wrote.

"I don't know, Blake. The whole thing feels overly simplistic, doesn't it?" She shakes her head. "And besides, being popular and not being bullied are two different things. There's not enough of a correlation there."

"But—I really think it can work, Priya." *It* is *working*, I add silently.

"Tell you what," she says. "How about I send this data to myself and go over it more carefully tonight, see if there's anything usable there. But for now, we brainstorm other ideas, okay?"

"I—"

Before I can stop her, she's already sent a link to herself. Just like that. Oh no. I can't have her reading the spreadsheet again. It won't take her long to figure out that half of it is about her!

"You know what, you're right!" I cry. "Forget all about my data. I'll do something else. Whatever you want. After all, you know how to pick a winning topic!" My voice is so high that I sound like a panicked bird.

Priya studies me, clearly puzzled by my sudden change of heart. But then she must decide it's not worth trying to figure me out, because she shrugs and says, "Well, I've heard kids complaining about the new recycling bins. What if you did something about that?"

"About recycling?"

"You could show how biodegradable different common lunchroom trash items are. That way people will think twice about the things they're throwing away."

"That sounds . . . smelly."

Priya nods. "Maybe. But also important, right?"

Honestly, I think it sounds smelly *and* kind of boring—not to mention gross. But at this point, it's better than Priya finding out the details of my experiment, so I say, "Um, yeah. That might be okay."

"Good," she says. "Let's start working on it."

"Now?"

"Why not? Do you have something better to do?"

I hesitate, thinking of my parents downstairs. Knowing Dad, he probably paused the movie in the hopes that we'd change our minds and come watch.

"Remember what I said on the first day of science club?" Priya asks. "We work hard, even on weekends."

"What about the playing hard part?" I ask. I haven't seen much of that so far.

Priya shrugs. "That's more of Owen's thing," she says. "So, are you ready?"

I bite back a sigh. "Sure." Who knew that my popularity plan would involve spending my Friday night researching trash?

CHAPTER 15

Kat and I are supposed to see each other on Saturday afternoon, but she sends me a message after lunch to cancel.

Everything okay? I ask.

Fine. Just have to work on stuff for the exhibit, she writes back.

I frown. *I thought you were all done?*

A long pause. *Not yet,* she writes back. Then she adds, *I told you the show's next month, Oct 12, right?*

Yup! On my calendar! I write back. *Should I dress up?*

Weirdly, she doesn't respond.

I try to tell myself it's nothing. Sometimes Kat can get a little intense when she's really into an art project, the same way I get when I'm doing an experiment. But

I keep thinking there's something else going on. I wish she'd tell me what it was.

Only after I toss my phone on my bed do I realize that I haven't even told her about my date with Owen. It's weird that after years of spending practically every minute together, there are entire things Kat and I don't know about each other's lives now. I guess that was bound to happen once we started going to different schools, but it still feels strange.

A few hours later, I go downstairs to help Maisie with dinner since it's our day of the week to cook. Mom is working a fundraiser and Dad is out biking with Uncle Joe, so it's just the two of us.

"Hey, stranger," Maisie says, handing me some carrots to peel. "Haven't seen you around much."

I'm surprised to realize it's true. Usually, I'm the one hanging out here after school while Maisie goes to a million clubs and parties. But she's been home a lot more lately, unless she's at her study group. And I'm always doing science club stuff. Or out with Owen.

"So I had a date yesterday." I try to sound casual,

but my voice shakes with excitement. Normally I'd never tell my sister about something like this, but I have to share it with someone!

Maisie's face lights up. "Really? With Parker?"

I blink. "Why do you think it was with Parker?"

"I've seen how you look at him," she says, wiggling her eyebrows. "He's really cute."

"He is," I admit. "But no. It was with Owen Campbell."

"Oh, Wyatt's brother?" She sounds surprised. "He doesn't really seem like your type."

"Are you kidding? He's a total science nerd. Of course he's my type!"

"I guess. And I could be wrong about him. It's just . . . he's never been all that friendly to me."

I can imagine that. He probably thinks Maisie is an airhead or something, but I'm sure he'd feel differently if he got to know her. She might not be out there changing the world with science, but she's certainly changing it with kindness. She spent every Saturday last spring helping out at a local food pantry. Not even Priya could look down on that.

"Owen takes a while to warm up to people, that's all," I tell her.

"So how did the date go?" she asks.

"Good, I think." I focus on my carrots for a minute. "Um, Maisie. How do you know if a guy wants you to be his girlfriend?"

She gives me a little smile, like she thinks my question is cute. But if anyone knows the answer, it's Maisie. She's had a string of adoring boyfriends since sixth grade. And, of course, she's managed to stay friends with them all.

"Well, sometimes he asks you. Or sometimes you ask him. But most of the time, I think you just hang out a bunch and then it kind of happens."

"That doesn't sound very scientific," I say.

Maisie chuckles. "It's definitely not. But don't worry about it! Hanging out with boys is meant to be fun. You're not supposed to be checking stuff off a list."

Of course, that's exactly what I'm trying to do, but I'm not going to admit that to my sister. "Anyway. How's stuff at your new school? Are they still banning you from wearing glitter?"

I expect her to at least crack a smile. But instead she shrugs and says, "I'm getting used to it."

That doesn't sound like Maisie's usual positive attitude at all. "Is everything okay?"

"It's fine!" she says as she puts a pot of water on to boil.

But I know that "fine." I use it all the time when I'm trying to convince myself that it's true.

"No, really. What's up?" I ask.

She sighs. "St. Mary's is so . . . serious," she says. "At Hemlock the classes were hard too. But at St. Mary's, everyone studies *all the time*. I haven't been invited to a single party since school started. I feel like I'm at a convent!"

"Well, it *is* a Catholic school," I joke. "But three weeks without any parties does sound pretty terrible by your standards."

Maisie snorts. "Anyway, I'm sure I'll make friends eventually. Everyone is nice and everything, but they kind of make me feel . . . stupid."

"You, stupid? No way!" Maisie might not be a nerd like I am, but she's always been smart in her own way. Mom calls it "emotional intelligence."

"I know I'm not," Maisie says. "And I did get a B-plus on a quiz yesterday. I guess all the studying is paying off."

"That's great," I say. It's funny to hear my sister talking about grades while I'm talking about boyfriends. It's like we've switched places or something!

CHAPTER 16

On Monday, I find Owen waiting for me at my locker after fourth period. "Want to walk to lunch together?" he asks.

I nod, breathless. He's never done this before. What does it mean?

As we walk down the hall together, kids smile at us or wave. I spot a couple of sixth grade girls wearing neon safety glasses in their hair like headbands, just like mine. I've only been at Lincoln for three weeks, but I suddenly realize that this place has been feeling less and less strange lately. I already feel safer here than I ever did at Hemlock.

As we head down the stairs toward the cafeteria, Owen says, "Did you hear? There's a new jock in town."

"Oh yeah? Who?"

He shrugs. "I haven't met her yet, but Priya told me. I guess this girl instantly bonded with Parker's crowd."

I swallow. I haven't spoken to Parker or Ashleigh since I blew off soccer practice on Friday. I got to the bus as late as possible this morning to avoid them.

We walk into the lunchroom, and I'm stunned when all eyes turn toward us. As if two Important People walked in the door. It's the most amazing feeling, to have kids looking at me for the right reasons rather than for the wrong ones.

I usually avoid even glancing at Parker and Ashleigh's table, but this time I'm curious about the new girl, so I look over—and freeze.

"That must be her," I hear Owen say. "Wow, she doesn't look like a jock. I'm pretty sure my dad has that same Wonder Woman shirt. And what's up with the rainbow hair?"

I know that shirt. I know that colorful hair. I know that girl.

"Kat?" I whisper.

"Lily!" she cries out, loud enough for everyone to

hear. Then she rushes over and throws her arms around me. "Oops, I mean *Blake*! I've been looking for you all day, but this school is huge!"

"Wh-what are you doing here?" I manage to say when she finally steps back.

"I wanted to surprise you. I go here now!"

I blink at her and then blink some more, trying to put the words into some kind of order that will make sense. But they don't. "What are you talking about? You said you'd never leave Hemlock."

"Well, things change," she says. She turns toward Owen, who I realize is still standing next to me. "Hey, I'm Kat. Blake's best friend. You must be Owen."

He gives her an uncertain smile. He's probably wondering how she knows his name when he's never even heard of her.

"Well, if you're Blake's friend, I guess you should come sit with us," Owen says. Then he gives me a little nod and heads over to our table.

Finally it sinks in. Kat is here, at Lincoln. This should be good news. This is what I've wanted all along, to have my best friend with me. And I *am* glad to see her, but . . . Kat isn't exactly known for being subtle. This could put my whole experiment at risk.

The first thing I need to do is get her sitting with the right people. "Come on. My table's this way."

"But what about . . . ?" She glances back at Ashleigh and Parker, who are watching the whole scene.

I can't let her stay and sit with them, or Priya will never let Kat into the group. "I'll help you move your stuff," I say quickly.

Kat's smile fades. "Ashleigh and Parker were so nice to me this morning. And Hector and Jayla seem great. Am I really supposed to ditch them?"

"They'll understand," I assure her, hoping I'm right. "Come on."

"I can't believe how weird this place is. I had to ask permission to use the bathroom!" Kat says as we start walking. "But the no-uniform life is awesome!"

"Hey, guys," I mumble when we get to Ashleigh and Parker's table.

"We missed you at soccer, Blake," Parker says. "Are you still on the team?"

I gulp. "Um, no. It turns out I . . . I don't really

have time." I can feel Ashleigh staring at me, but I don't make eye contact with her. "Hey, listen, Kat's going to sit with me today. But, um, thanks for showing her around."

"It was nice to meet you," Hector says, flashing Kat a shy little smile.

"We'll see you at practice," Ashleigh says.

I think she's talking to me, until Kat answers, "Yeah, see you on Wednesday."

"You're doing soccer?" I ask Kat as we walk away. "I thought you hated sports."

"I hate *equestrian*," she says. "But soccer sounds okay. And it doesn't interfere with the art club."

"Don't forget about the science club," I remind her. "That takes up a lot of time too. It's kind of late for you to start a showcase project, but maybe we could team up or something."

"Science club? Me?" Kat snorts. "You know that's not my thing."

I pull her to a stop by the cafeteria windows. "Kat, you know about my experiment," I whisper. "You know how things work here. If you want to be part of the right crowd, you have to follow my lead, okay?"

"But—"

"Can you just trust me? I know what I'm doing!"

She sighs. I can see that she wants to argue—doing what other people say isn't exactly her favorite. But finally she nods and says, "Okay, I'll try."

CHAPTER 17

As I go to meet Kat in the lobby before her first science club meeting, I'm excited and nervous. Having her around could be a great way of testing out my popularity findings on someone else, to really confirm that they work. I only wish there weren't so many things that could go wrong.

I can't stop thinking about how weird it was to have Kat at lunch with us today. She kept talking about her comic books, which I could tell Priya wasn't too impressed with. But at least she agreed to come to the science club meeting. Kat is smart and funny. I'm sure once the other kids get to know her, she'll fit right in.

When I pass by Parker's locker, I purposely slow

down. Even if he and I aren't really hanging out anymore, I can usually count on his adorable smile. But this time he's not smiling. He seems upset as he pulls a textbook out of his locker. It looks like it's been coated with something—glue, maybe? I guess the remedial kids have struck again.

I hesitate, wondering if I should go over and offer to help. But then Ashleigh appears in the hallway, and I hurry away, sure she won't want me around.

When I get to the lobby, I find Kat talking to Hector. The two of them are bonding over their love of a manga series she's always trying to get me to read. I can't believe it. I warned Kat not to hang out with Parker and his friends. Why is she standing around with Hector for all to see?

"Kat," I say, grabbing her arm. "I need you." Then I drag her away as fast as possible.

"What's wrong?" she asks.

"Nothing. You might not want to hang out with Hector too much, that's all."

I can tell she wants to argue, but instead she groans

and says, "Fine." Then she follows me down the hall that leads to Miss Turner's room.

Now that we're finally alone, I have a chance to ask the question that's been burning inside me all afternoon. "So what happened at Hemlock? I thought you were going to stick it out there until the bitter end."

Kat shrugs. "Lincoln's art club is supposed to be a lot better. That's how I managed to convince my mom to let me transfer here."

She might have convinced her mom, but I know better. "It was Queen Courtenay, wasn't it? She did something?"

"Of course she did," Kat says with a bitter laugh. "She's always doing *something*."

It's obvious she doesn't want to tell me, but I simply stay quiet and wait until finally she sighs and adds, "She destroyed my drawing, the one I was supposed to have in the art show."

My mouth sags open. "She *destroyed* it?"

"Yup. Put it in the paper shredder and then claimed it was an accident," Kat says. "It was right before our teacher was supposed to send the pieces over to the gallery. I had to redo the whole thing in two days."

"Wow." It's all I can say, because I'm so stunned. I guess being away from Queen Courtenay for a little while has made me forget how evil she can be.

"That's when I realized I was done with Hemlock," Kat says. "I didn't care if she messed up my *life* at school, but my *art*? No way."

I nod. I guess we all have our breaking points, even Kat.

"But also," Kat goes on, "I missed you. I wanted to be here with my best friend."

Suddenly I feel awful about how freaked out I've been that Kat might mess up my experiment.

"I'm so sorry about your art project," I tell her. "But I'm really glad you're here."

"Come on," she says, looping her arm through mine. "Don't want to be late for science club!"

Things go okay at first. When Priya asks about Kat's showcase project, I say brightly, "I was thinking that Kat and I could team up on my compost research, and she'll design the poster."

"I'm not much of a scientist, so yeah, that sounds good," Kat says.

Someone behind me gasps. Then the room goes silent for a moment, as if everyone's too shocked to speak.

"If you're not much of a scientist, then why are you here?" Priya asks finally.

"Because Blake asked me to come," Kat says lightly.

What is she doing?

"And," she adds, oblivious, "I wanted to check this out and see if it's something I'd want to do."

Priya's eyebrows shoot up. "*We* pick *you*, not the other way around."

"Oh yeah?" Now Kat sounds serious—she does love a challenge.

"It's just that we have some really big goals," I jump in. "So you pretty much have to be all in. But that's fine, right, Kat? You're all in?"

I give her a pleading look. Doesn't she understand how important this is to me? To us?

She looks at me for a moment. Finally she shrugs. "Yeah, okay," she says. "But there's no way I'm wearing a lab coat or anything."

Ugh. Maybe getting Kat to fit into my new life is going to be harder than I thought.

At dinner, Mom goes on and on about how glad she is to finally have the whole family together at the table. "This house has been full of passing ships lately!" she says.

It's true. Dad's really stepped up the training, since there's less than a month left until the half marathon, Maisie's been spending almost all her time studying, and Mom has been working more than usual.

But for some reason, Mom singles *me* out. "You're never home anymore, Blake. Always off with your new friends. I'm glad that you're being so social, honey, but we miss you."

"It's just been busy with the showcase," I say. "Once that's over, things will calm down." I figure now is not a good time to mention that Priya really wants the club to start applying for grants in the spring, to try to get funding for some of our projects, which will probably take up a lot of time too.

"At least you have Kat at school with you now," Dad chimes in. "We've missed seeing her." He has an ice pack on each knee and a heating pad on his neck. Plus athletic bandages on both elbows. It's amazing all his limbs are still attached.

I nod. I've missed Kat too. I just wish having her at Lincoln didn't feel so complicated.

"Maisie," Mom says, "I heard you have some big news for us."

My sister beams. "I got an A-minus on my math test!"

"Good for you!" Dad cries. "Isn't that great, Blake?"

"Yeah," I say. Then, because everyone is looking at me as if I should sound more excited, I add, "Good job."

I can't remember Maisie ever making a big deal out of her grades before. But she has been studying a lot. I guess she's happy to have that work paying off. It's just funny that no one seems to care that I get As all the time.

After dinner, I'm surprised when Maisie pulls me aside. "Can we go talk on the porch?" she asks.

"Um, yeah. Okay." Her serious face is making me nervous. "What's up?" I ask when we're sitting out on the three-season porch. It's a little chilly out here, but not so bad once you snuggle up under a blanket on one of the wicker armchairs.

She gives me a long look before saying, "I was talking to Maya—you know, Parker's sister? And she said that your friends have been giving Parker a hard time."

I shake my head. "What are you talking about?"

"There have been a few incidents, I guess, but she said the most recent thing was that someone glued his science textbook shut."

"And you think my friends had something to do with that?" I ask. "No way. I mean, there are pranks at school, but I heard it's probably the remedials doing it."

"The whats?" Maisie says, frowning. "You mean the stupid kids? Like me?"

"No! I didn't say—"

"Why would they prank Parker? He seems really nice. What do they have against him?"

"I don't know," I admit. "But it wasn't my friends. They'd never do that to someone."

"Are you sure about that?"

"Yes!" The way she's acting is so strange. Since when has she ever accused anyone of anything? She's usually all about giving people the benefit of the doubt. "I don't get it. Why are you suddenly so down on my new friends? Unless . . . you're jealous!"

She blinks. "What?"

"For once, I'm the one with friends and you're not. You hate it that I'm more popular than you are." It makes sense, the way she's been so weird talking about her school and how judgmental she's being about my friends.

Maisie laughs in disbelief. "That's ridiculous," she says. "You're the one who—"

She cuts herself off, but I know what she was about to say. I'm the one who should be jealous of her. And yes, that's been true for years. But not now.

"I don't need to be jealous of you," I tell her. "Not anymore." Then I stomp back into the house.

CHAPTER 18

On Wednesday, I'm surprised to see Ashleigh waiting at my locker after school.

"Did we do something wrong?" she asks.

"What do you mean?"

"Everything seemed great, and then suddenly you quit the soccer team and stopped talking to us. It doesn't make sense."

I swallow. "I'm sorry. I just don't really have time with—"

"I don't get it," she cuts in. "I don't get why you would pick them over us." She turns to walk away, but then she adds, "Do you know that I used to go to sleepovers at Priya's house all the time when we were little? She'd invite all the girls in our class."

"Really?" I can't imagine it. What did Ashleigh and Priya even talk about?

"That was before her brother turned into a model citizen and Priya turned into his clone." She shakes her head. "I don't even remember her liking science back then. She had her heart set on being a singer."

"I've never heard her talk about music," I say. But then I remember her singing in my room, and what a good voice she had.

"Yeah, it's weird, right?" Ashleigh says. "How someone can turn into a completely different person."

The way she looks at me makes me think we're not talking about Priya anymore.

"I really am sorry about soccer," I say.

But Ashleigh shakes her head. "It's not about soccer, Blake. I thought we were friends. But I guess I didn't really know you at all." Then she walks away.

After school, Kat and I walk the couple of miles back to my house to work on our science project. I come up with some ideas for designs for the poster, but Kat is super quiet. In fact, now that I think about it, she's been quiet all day. We don't have any classes together, but she hardly said a word during lunch.

"Are you okay?" I finally ask her after we get to my house and go up to my room.

Kat sighs and shuts my bedroom door. "How much do you really know about Priya and Owen?"

"What do you mean?"

"Well, it's just . . . I was getting such a weird vibe off them. So I decided to do some digging, into the club and them. And I found something."

Suddenly there's a hollow feeling in my stomach. "What did you find?"

Kat shakes her head. "It's probably better if I show you." She takes her phone out of her bag and starts scrolling. "You know how you said that your sister's drink exploded all over her at that pool party?"

"Yeah. Why?"

"There's a channel with videos of science pranks. It's made by someone at our school who goes by the name ScienceOwl. Look at this one."

She turns her phone for me to see. The shaky video shows a familiar kitchen. Whoever is holding the camera must have been in the hallway. A figure moves through the kitchen, carrying a bottle. He places it on the counter in front of two kids and then he leaves.

Everyone's faces are blurred out, but it's obvious that it's Maisie and Wyatt Campbell hanging out at the pool party.

After a moment, the girl (Maisie) picks up the bottle and opens it, and the lemonade starts pouring all over her. She jumps back and shrieks. A minute later, another girl who looks like a miniature Maisie rushes over to her. It takes me a second to realize that the second girl is me!

Then the video cuts to a picture of a cartoon owl with the sound of a distorted voice in the background.

"Success!" the voice says. "The bottle was actually meant for the guy, but the prank worked just the same! Want to try this at home? Here's how." Then the person launches into a cartoon demonstration of how if you poke holes in a bottle, the surface tension will keep it from leaking until it's opened. And then when you unscrew the cap —bam!

The video ends, and I can only stand there, speechless.

"Lily?" Kat says finally. "Are you okay?"

"It was Owen. He made that bottle explode all over Maisie."

"Yeah. But it wasn't meant for her. He was trying to get that guy to pick it up, but Maisie got it instead."

"That was Wyatt, Owen's older brother." I shake my head. "But . . . why would he do that?" I think back to that day. Owen did seem kind of annoyed with his brother for breaking his microscope, but would he really prank him as some sort of revenge?

"He did it because he's a jerk," Kat says. "They all are. That's what I'm trying to tell you! There's something wrong with that club of yours."

I turn to her. "What are you talking about? Why is this the club's fault?"

"Pulling science pranks on people? That's obviously what they do for fun. The next video is all about how to make a milk carton explode."

My stomach plummets. The milk carton attack.

"But . . . but they're not like that," I say. "Priya hates 'junk science,' and Owen is—"

166

"A horrible human being."

"He's not!" I insist. "He just has a grudge against Parker. Owen told me that Parker and his friends bullied him when they were younger. Obviously he still hasn't gotten over it."

Kat's eyes widen. "Are you defending him?"

"No. Not . . . not exactly."

"And what about Priya?" Kat says.

"What about her?"

"She might not be into junk science, but someone was holding the camera when Owen was bringing the lemonade over. You told me she was there that day. Don't you think it was her?"

Suddenly I remember what Priya said the first time I met her at the pool party. She was looking for Owen because he wanted her help with something. Was this it? Were they planning this prank together?

My head is throbbing. This doesn't fit with any of my data. How could they be behind all the pranks at school? The day the spaghetti exploded, Priya was sitting right next to me! And Owen . . .

I swallow, the realization sinking in. Owen

wasn't there. Bree told me he was meeting with Miss Turner. But maybe that was only an excuse.

How could I be so blind? Owen told me he hates Parker and his whole crowd. And it's obvious the science club kids can get away with anything!

"So," Kat says, "what are you going to do?"

"Me?" I squeak. "What *can* I do? Ditch Priya and Owen and everyone else? They're what's been keeping me safe at Lincoln!"

"Is that really all you care about? Being *safe*?" She practically spits the word.

"Of course not. But—"

"Look, Lily. I'm sorry, but if you keep hanging out with them, then we can't be friends anymore."

Kat's words feel like a punch to the gut. "Wh-what? But you're my best friend."

"Then you need to get them to stop." Her face is dead serious. This is not a fight she's going to back down from.

I nod. "Okay. Okay." Priya and Owen aren't evil, not like Queen Courtenay. I'm sure there's a way to reason with them. "I'll talk to them. I promise."

CHAPTER 19

So, is Kat liking Lincoln?" Mom asks me during our Friday-night dinner. For once, we're all home to keep up the tradition.

"I guess so." I haven't really spoken to her the past couple of days. She's been lying low ever since our talk. I know she's waiting for me to confront Owen and Priya, but I haven't been able to figure out a way to do it.

"Is Kat going to be part of your little clique now?" Maisie shoots from across the table. "Just start doing what everyone else is doing?"

This might be the first time Maisie's actually said anything directly to me since we fought. Clearly, she's still mad at me.

"Isn't there a study group you need to get to?" I shoot back.

Maisie rolls her eyes and grabs her plate. Then she storms into the kitchen and goes upstairs to her room.

"What was that about?" Dad calls from the floor. His back is hurting from his workout yesterday, so he's sprawled on the kitchen tile with cushions under his head and knees. Mom put a plate of food on the floor for him to pick at and water that he can sip through a straw.

"Did you and Maisie have a fight?" Mom adds, sounding utterly confused. Because my sister and I never fight. Maisie is the most forgiving person in the world. Or at least she used to be. These days, I'm starting to feel like I barely know her anymore.

"Not a fight, exactly," I say. "It's just . . . don't you think she's been really different since she started at St. Mary's? So serious and stuff."

"Yes," Mom says, "but that was one reason she wanted to go there. Now that she's thinking ahead to college, she wants to feel more challenged."

"Okay, but . . . a school that won't even let her wear glitter? How is that a good fit for her?"

Mom laughs. "Maisie's glittery enough on the inside. Besides, you've changed too, haven't you?"

"No, I haven't. I mean, okay, my name. But I'm just trying to make, you know, improvements."

"That's the thing about improving something," Dad calls up to me. "A lot of times there's nothing wrong with the original." Just then his phone beeps and he groans when he reads the message. "Joe wants to do another long run tomorrow. At six a.m."

"Tomorrow?" Mom asks. "But you were going to help me bring over those book donations."

"Oh, right," Dad says. "I'll, um . . . I'll see if he can do it earlier."

"Any earlier and it'll still be night," I point out.

Dad chuckles. "That's what headlamps are for!" Mom looks worried, so he adds, "I'll be back in plenty of time to help you, Jen." Then he groans and grumbles as he heaves himself off the floor to go put his dish in the sink.

"Here, I'll do that," I say, rushing over to him.

Dad laughs. "Never get old, okay? You won't like it."

But we both know his age isn't the problem. He was fine until he started training for the half marathon. I don't know why he lets my uncle push him around so much. I guess maybe he still thinks he has something to prove after all these years.

"Dad," I say, leading him over to the couch. "You don't need to be a new-and-improved version of yourself, either."

He gives me a small smile. "Thanks, kiddo," he says. But I can't tell if he believes me.

On Monday, Kat refuses to eat lunch with me, insisting that I need to talk to Owen and Priya first. As she goes to sit with Hector, I head to my table, knowing I need to confront Owen and get it over with. I figure since he's the one who posted the video, I should start with him.

It takes half of lunch for Priya and Owen to stop chattering about science club business, but finally she turns to talk to Bree, and I see my chance.

"Hey, Owen," I say softly. "Can I talk to you about something?"

"What's up?" he says around a bite of his sandwich.

I take a big breath and say, "I saw the video from the pool party. I know about the pranks."

He doesn't react at first, just keeps chewing. Then he says, "Okay."

"That's it? You're not even going to try to explain why you made lemonade explode all over my sister?"

His eyebrows go up in surprise. "That girl was your sister?"

"Yes. She's like the nicest person in the world, and you soaked her."

"It was an accident. I was trying to get back at—"

"Wyatt. I know. And I know you're the one who made that milk explode, and you were behind the glued textbook and the spaghetti prank too. What I don't get is *why*."

Owen lets out a slow breath and leans back in his chair. "I don't expect you to understand.

When kids mess with you, it gets under your skin."

"I do understand! I was *tortured* at my old school. That's why I came here. This one girl at Hemlock, she and her friends are totally evil. But you're not like that."

Owen looks down at his sandwich, not saying anything for a moment. "That girl at your old school," he says softly. "If you had a chance to get back at her, wouldn't you take it?"

I hesitate. Because I've dreamed about doing exactly that so many times. The only difference is that I'll probably never get the chance. But Owen can, and he's going for it. I guess I can understand that, even if I don't like it.

"Maybe," I admit. "But you can't keep getting back at them forever. When will you be done?"

"I have two more pranks planned, and that's it."

"When?"

He doesn't answer at first, only takes a sip of his water. Then he says, "How about we make a deal?"

"A deal?"

"If you help me with my last two pranks, I'll help

you get back at the girl who tortured you. We can make her pay for what she did."

I stare at him for a moment, not sure what to say. But really, there's only one answer, isn't there? This is far too good of an offer for me to pass up.

"Deal."

CHAPTER 20

The plan is simple. The next day, I stop Hector outside the cafeteria before lunch and ask him some made-up question about our math homework. While he's distracted, Owen switches out the pack of Oreos in Hector's bag that he always brings for lunch. Then I just have to tell Hector "thanks" and walk away.

It goes perfectly.

A few minutes later, I sit next to Owen at lunch as he covertly records the whole thing on his phone. We watch Hector open the pack of Oreos and pop one in his mouth. There's a moment of surprise on his face as he realizes that the filling isn't cream—it's toothpaste.

Then he spits out the Oreo and starts coughing.

Kat pats him on the back, like she thinks he's choking. But then Hector starts laughing and holds up the Oreos to show everyone.

The other kids at the table glance around, as if looking for the culprit, so Owen and I pretend we're deep in conversation.

When I glance back, I gasp to see Hector opening the pack of Oreos again. He shrugs and pops another one in his mouth.

"I guess he likes them," Owen says to me.

I giggle. "Gross."

"See?" Owen says. "That wasn't so bad, was it?"

"No," I admit. It wasn't. Actually, it was kind of fun.

I notice Priya looking right at us. It's obvious she knows what we've been up to and that she doesn't approve.

"A food prank? Really?" she says. "Isn't that a little low, even for you, Owen?"

Owen's cheeks flush. "Don't worry, we'll step it up next time. Won't we, Blake?"

Right—I promised him I'd help with *two* pranks.

But if that one is anything like this, it's not nearly as bad as I was imagining.

"Yeah," I say. "We'll come up with something good."

Kat sends me a message that night. *Any idea why Hector's Oreos were weirdly minty at lunch today?*

I stare at those words for a while, trying to think how to respond. She probably doesn't know that I was involved in the prank. If she did, she wouldn't be speaking to me at all. But there's still an accusation behind her question.

What would she think if she knew that my teaming up with Owen meant a chance to get back at Queen Courtenay? Would she understand? After all, I bet Kat dreams of revenge as much as I do. If anything, I want to do this for both of us—what Courtenay did to Kat's art project was *horrible*. She was so awful that Kat and I both switched schools! If anyone deserves to be pranked, it's Queen Courtenay.

But these days, it feels like I don't know how Kat is going to react to anything I do or say. So finally I simply write back, *I'm working on it.*

Luckily, Kat is super busy with art and soccer, so the rest of the week actually feels pretty normal. I go to school, hang out with Owen and Priya, and work on my science project.

I don't *love* testing different biodegradable and compostable lunch items to see how long it takes them to break down, but it's going pretty well. My parents haven't been thrilled about the smell in the shed—which I convinced them I needed for the setup—so I keep reminding them that science is often stinky. And if I do a good enough job, I'll get to meet Exploding Emma! I haven't had much time to watch her videos lately, but the chance to see her in person is at least as motivating as knowing how impressed Priya will be with my results.

My compost experiment might be messy, but at least my popularity one is going great. Despite the Kat situation and the pranks—which are really just hiccups in the larger scheme of things—I'm right where I want to be: I'm part of an entourage, I have a (maybe?) boyfriend, and I can't even remember the last time I had to recite the periodic table to myself. Plus, my social calendar is jam-packed, and I've started a fashion trend with my safety glasses. Five Factors of Popularity? Check, check, check, check, *and* check!

I'm feeling so confident, in fact, that when Priya and I get together to work on our projects after school one day, I dare to ask her about what Ashleigh told me.

"Is it true you used to want to be a singer?" She's been humming along with the music and tapping her toes since she got here, almost like she can't help it.

Priya sort of jumps at the question, which is such a change from her usual indifferent attitude that *I* almost jump. "Who told you that?" she snaps.

"Um, I can't remember. I just—I thought I heard it somewhere."

She shrugs, and the alarmed look on her face settles back into her normal cool-and-collected expression. "Yeah, when I was a little kid, I was convinced I was going to be a pop star." She rolls her eyes. "Pretty pathetic, right?"

"No, why?"

"Because that's not a real dream. It's not something you can actually *do* with your life. Not like science."

"Okay . . . but you could do both, couldn't you? Be a singer and a scientist?"

She snorts. "My parents would love that."

I think back to what she said about her parents giving her science-y jewelry. I thought it was because they understood her, but maybe it's actually the opposite.

"Are they really into you becoming a scientist?" I ask.

She shrugs again. "Not exactly. It's more like they're really into me being as amazing as Ravi. If he wins an award, they expect me to win it too."

Boy, does *that* sound familiar. "My mom is kind of like that about my sister and me," I admit. "I think she's still hoping I'll magically turn into Maisie one day. But my sister and I are into different things, so at least we're not really competing with each other."

"Luckily I'm as good at science as my brother is," Priya says, but she doesn't sound like someone who feels lucky.

"You're also good at singing," I point out.

"Maybe, but I've never won any awards for it, so what's the point?"

"Because then you might actually be happy?" The

more time I spend with Priya, the more miserable she seems. I've never really heard her laugh, never seen her genuinely smile. She's so serious and critical all the time.

Priya swallows, and for a second, it looks like she might say something real. But then she rolls her eyes again. "Come on. Let's get back to work."

For a minute I just watch her entering in data for the carbon footprint project she's been working on. Based on her results so far, the project is amazing. If she can put it all together, she'll definitely be a showcase winner again. And please her parents, I bet. And maybe even feel good?

"What?" she finally says, looking up.

"Oh, nothing. It's just—I also heard that Parker and Owen used to be friends?" If I can't tell her what I'm really thinking—and I definitely can't—at least I can research *that* mystery.

This question doesn't seem to surprise her at all. "We all used to be friends, I guess, when we were little." It reminds me of what Ashleigh said about going to sleepovers at Priya's house.

"So what happened?"

"Owen's like an elephant. He never forgets things. If you get on his bad side, it's pretty hard to get off of it."

"What about you?" I dare to ask. "Do you ever hold grudges against people?"

"Nah," she says. "Life's too short."

"Then why do you help Owen with his pranks?" They're not exactly Priya's style.

"Same reason as you, I guess."

I wonder for a second if they have some sort of deal too.

But then she adds, "I remember what it was like, before we were popular. Kids ignored me since I was so quiet. But Owen always stood out. He was smarter than pretty much anyone else in our grade, and he'd get so excited about stuff that other kids thought was nerdy. They were always making fun of him, always messing with him." She shakes her head. "Then we got to Lincoln and took over the science club, and suddenly kids who'd been so mean were worshipping us. They were acting like the stuff they did to him was forgotten."

"But Owen doesn't forget," I say.

"Exactly. It's weird, but I think the pranks are a way for him to get over everything. That's why I've been helping him make those videos, even if I think they're a waste of perfectly good science."

I wonder if Owen *will* ever get over it. He's the one who said he doesn't think people can change. Will he always see Parker as the boy who stood by while he was bullied, no matter how much time goes by?

But then again, I totally get it. The more I think about it, the more I can't wait until I'm basking in Queen Courtenay's humiliation. After everything she's done to Kat and me—just imagining how we're going to get back at her makes me feel better every day. The first little prank on Hector was fine. Fun, even.

So. Maybe Owen and I *are* alike, and not just on paper.

CHAPTER 21

Owen is waiting for me at my locker before the next science club meeting.

"Here," he says, handing me a file folder.

Inside I find several pieces of paper: a list of new prank ideas; info about Queen Courtenay, including her schedule; and even pictures of her that look like they're from her social media accounts.

"Where did you get this?" I ask.

"Not hard to find. She's everywhere." He leans over and points to her schedule. "Check it out. Lincoln is playing Hemlock's soccer team the day of the Science Showcase, and she's one of the goalies. So all we have to do is win the showcase and then go to the game afterward and destroy her."

I swallow. Owen doesn't know that I was supposed to be at that game, as part of Lincoln's team. I forgot about the fact that our school will be playing Hemlock this season. Ugh. What am I supposed to do? Kat will be at the game. If she catches me helping Owen with a prank, she'll flip out. Even if the target is Queen Courtenay.

"Maybe we can find another time?" I say. "You know, with not as many people around?"

But Owen shakes his head. "No, this is perfect. The more people the better. Then she'll really be humiliated."

I chew on my lip.

"That's what you want, right?" Owen goes on. "To embarrass her the way she embarrassed you? You're not chickening out, are you?"

"No!" I say. "No, you're right. Let's do it at the game." I'll just have to figure out a way to do it without making things even worse with Kat.

"Platinum," Owen says. Then he glances around, as if he's making sure no one else is nearby, and adds, "Hey, I wanted to ask you if you were going to the dance on Friday?"

I've seen the homecoming dance flyers around school, but I've been kind of ignoring them. I know everything in my research has told me that dances are important social events, and I should be going for the experiment. But to be honest, I'm still not over the last school dance I went to.

"Um, dances aren't really my thing," I say.

"Oh. Well, this one is pretty fun. Everyone gets dressed up and stuff. Priya usually boycotts the dances because they use plastic cups and plates, but it's actually a good time."

"Th-that does sound fun," I say slowly.

"So, what do you think? Maybe we could meet up there?"

I almost fall over. I can't believe it. He wants us to go to the dance *together*? "Yes!" I cry. Then I pull myself together and add, "I mean, yeah. I could do that."

But inside, I'm still squealing. This is the crowning achievement of my experiment! Not only will I be going to a major social event, but I'll be going with the most popular boy in my grade!

* * *

The next prank is on Jayla. I guess she offended Owen at some point too—I'm not bothering to keep track anymore. I'm just glad that this will be the last one, and I hope it goes as easily as the Oreos.

But coming up with the prank isn't quite as easy as last time. The only class that Jayla, Owen, and I have together is English, so it'll have to be then. We try to think of something that will make a big impact but won't get us in trouble.

"Maybe we can make her pen explode or something," Owen says when we're brainstorming at lunch.

"That could happen by itself," I point out. "She might not even realize it's a prank."

"That's true." He goes back to scrolling through notes on his phone of things he's pulled in the past, looking for inspiration.

I glance over his shoulder and notice Priya's name on the list. "Wait, you pranked Priya?" I whisper. She's on the other side of the table debating something with Ryder, not paying attention to us. Still, I don't want her to know we're talking about her.

"Nah," Owen says. "I'd never do that. But

sometimes I have really good ideas for how to mess with specific people, so I write them down, just in case." He smiles. "What, you've never thought about pranking any of your friends?"

"No!" I cry.

"You should. It's kind of fun."

I glance across the cafeteria to where Kat is sitting with Ashleigh and Hector again. She pulls her trusty bottle of ketchup out of her bag and puts some on her fries. As I watch her, an idea pops into my head.

"It probably wouldn't be hard to make ketchup explode," I say, half to myself.

Owen grins as he follows my gaze. "Not hard at all."

"You're right, this is fun," I say. "But you know I'd never actually do it, right?"

"Of course not. That doesn't mean you can't imagine."

We get back to brainstorming our prank on Jayla.

"Maybe we could do something with that lotion she's always using," Owen says finally. "It stinks up the room every single day."

"I think it smells nice, like cucumber," I say. But

he's right that Jayla *is* pretty predictable. At the start of English class, she almost always takes a small bottle of lotion out of her bag and rubs the stuff all over her hands. It might be our best bet.

"Let's do it this afternoon," Owen says once we've come up with the details of our plan. And like that, it's decided.

The setup is similar to the Oreo prank, but this time I need to cause a diversion so Owen can get into Jayla's backpack.

I call Jayla over before English class starts and ask her a question about our homework. She seems a little surprised that I'm actually talking to her, but she's nice enough to explain the assignment to me. As she's finishing up, I accidentally-on-purpose spill my water bottle all over the floor. Our teacher, Mr. Owusu, hands me some paper towels and—as predicted—Jayla helps me clean up the spill, while the other kids look on and giggle. This gives Owen time to squirt some Elmer's glue into the lotion bottle and put it back in Jayla's bag.

When the spilled water is cleaned up and Owen's

back in his seat, I give Jayla a bright smile and thank her for her help.

"No problem," she says before heading back to her desk. Phew. That wasn't bad at all.

But a few minutes later, as Mr. Owusu gives a lesson on the themes of good and evil in a story we're reading, a scream echoes through the room. I turn to see Jayla's hands coated in what looks like alien goo. The lotion and the glue have mixed together to form a gloppy green mess.

"Ew!" someone says. "What's wrong with your hands?"

I expect Jayla to realize it's a joke and maybe even laugh it off like Hector did. I mean, it *is* kind of funny.

But she sits in stunned silence for a second. Then she bursts into tears and runs out of the room.

Ashleigh jumps up. "I'll go check on her," she tells Mr. Owusu.

I glance over to see Owen's reaction, but he's busy copying down what's on the board—or at least pretending to.

When Ashleigh and Jayla come back a few minutes

later, Jayla's hands are back to normal and her tears are gone. But Ashleigh is clearly furious.

I feel horrible. I had no idea Jayla would *cry*. But I mean, who gets that upset about goo?

Jayla assures the teacher that everything is fine, then goes back to her seat as if nothing happened. So maybe she realized it wasn't that big a deal after all.

Across the room, Owen nods at his phone with a conspiratorial grin. I guess his plan to secretly film the whole thing worked out.

It might not be that funny, though, if he also filmed Jayla crying.

As I turn back to the board, I notice Mr. Owusu giving Owen a long look, his mouth in a tight line. I wait for him to say something, to accuse Owen. But instead he shakes his head slightly and returns to his lesson. Double phew.

When I get to my locker after the last bell, Owen is waiting for me.

"The video is platinum," he says. "Better than platinum. Titanium!"

"It's a good thing this was our last one, though. I think Mr. Owusu was suspicious."

But Owen only laughs. "Don't worry about it. The teachers are totally clueless." Then he leans in and gives me a kiss on the cheek, right in front of everyone. "Thanks for the help, Blake. You rock."

I don't see Kat after school, but before I go to bed that night, I get a text from her.

I heard there was another prank today. You said you'd make them stop.

I can't keep putting it off anymore. I have to come clean with Kat about the pranks. Now that it's just Queen Courtenay left, she'll have to understand.

When I dial her number, Kat answers with a surprised "Hello? Since when do you call me?"

It's true that we usually video chat rather than talk on the phone, but for some reason, I'd rather not see her face during this conversation.

"Look, there's something you should know," I say. And then I tell her about my deal with Owen.

When I'm done, there's silence on the other end. If

it weren't for the faint sound of music in the background, I'd think she'd hung up.

"I know that stuff with Hector and Jayla was silly," I go on, "but it was a means to an end, you know?"

More silence.

"Kat!" I cry. "This is it. We always said we wanted to get back at Courtenay, and now's our chance!"

"You said," Kat says softly.

"What?"

"*You* said you wanted to get back at her. You're the one who was joking about squeezing her head like it was slime."

"Because she's a monster!" I cry. "She deserves it."

"She *is* a monster, but the way you're talking . . ."

"What?" I demand.

But Kat doesn't answer my question. Instead, she says, "I'm sorry, Lily. You do what you want to Courtenay. I'm not going to help you."

Then she hangs up before I can say anything else.

CHAPTER 22

With only a couple of days until the dance, I need help preparing. And I know exactly who to ask.

Too bad she's barely speaking to me.

I figure the best way to butter up my sister is with something shiny, so when I get home from school on Wednesday, I make her some super-glittery "galaxy slime" and go present it to her as a peace offering.

"What?" she says when I knock on her door. She's slumped at her desk, practically drowning in textbooks. With midterms coming up, the house has been weirdly quiet. All Maisie does now is study—no music, no friends over, nothing.

"I brought you something that's good for stress," I say, holding out the slime.

She glances at it, and I can tell she's fighting with herself. She's still mad at me, but she does like shiny things. And squishing slime *is* pretty awesome.

"Thanks," she finally says, taking it. Then she turns back to her desk.

I know that's my cue to leave, but I linger in her doorway until she looks back up, her eyebrows raised.

"I just, um, was wondering if you could help me," I say. "There's this dance at school on Friday and . . . I need a dress."

Maisie sits back in her chair. "I'm really busy."

"I know. But it won't take a lot of time. I promise. I'm just totally clueless."

"Why not ask your friends?" she asks.

"You know Kat would put me in something blinding," I say, before realizing that she's not talking about Kat. She means my *new* friends. "And the others . . . I don't trust them the way I trust you."

At that, her expression softens a little. Progress!

"Please, Mais?" I beg. "I know you'll help me find something amazing. I tried googling homecoming dresses, but . . ."

Finally Maisie's composure cracks. "Of course you thought you could research your way through this! But fashion doesn't work that way."

"Okay, so can you show me how it does work?"

She sighs. "I guess I could use a break. Okay, come on." She sits me down on her bed and asks me a million questions about the dance: when it is, where it is, what colors I'm imagining.

"Colors?" I echo. "Like when I close my eyes, what colors do I see?"

She laughs. "No! What color do you want to wear?"

"Oh!" I snort. "See? This is why I need your help."

Once she's gotten my answers, she starts looking online. "Something like this," she finally decides, showing me a picture. "Or maybe something like this. Either one will be great." She turns to me, and she's actually smiling. "So who are you going to the dance with? Parker?"

"Um, no. Actually, I'm going with Owen."

Her smile fades. "Oh."

"You were kind of right about him and the other kids," I admit. "They *were* behind those pranks, but they're done pulling them now. It's over."

"So that's it?" Maisie asks. "You're going to forget that it happened?"

"What am I supposed to do?"

"Not go to the dance with Owen, for starters," Maisie says.

"It's not that simple. I need to go to the dance with him."

"*Need* to? Why?"

But how can I explain it to Maisie when she's never been picked on in her entire life? She won't understand about my experiment, about needing to be one of the popular kids, about staying safe. And part of me is embarrassed to admit that I had to come up with a whole experiment to help me accomplish things that come so easily to her.

"I just do, okay?" I insist.

Maisie shakes her head. "I don't get it. You've been acting so weird lately, Lily. It's like I have no idea who you are anymore."

"It's Blake, remember? And you don't know how hard middle school is, Maisie. If you're like me, you have to keep your head down or you'll start getting picked on."

She sighs. "I know life was rough for you at Hemlock—"

Suddenly something inside me snaps. "No, you don't know!" I cut in. "You have no idea! You were the queen of that place! It's different for me, okay? I have a chance to start over at Lincoln. I'm not going to ruin it!"

Before she can say anything else, I storm down the hall and lock myself in my room. I curl up on my bed, feeling shaken and sad.

But that doesn't make sense. My life is going perfectly! I have a group of friends who love science, just like I do, and Kat is at Lincoln, and I have a date to a dance! My experiment is totally working—better than I could have imagined. So what if I helped with a couple of little pranks? Soon I'll be able to put Queen Courtenay in her place and truly move on. I'll be Blake, once and for all: popular and safe and never bullied again. Science for the win!

Why can't Maisie see that? And why am I crying?

After a while, I calm down, wash my face, and ask Mom to take me dress shopping. She jumps at the chance, as if she's been waiting *years* for me to ask. And maybe she has, hoping I'd turn into a daughter she could actually relate to.

At the outdoor mall, I'm the one dragging Mom from store to store.

"What exactly is it that you're looking for?" she asks.

I try to remember the two styles that Maisie recommended, but it's pretty fuzzy. "Something blue," I say. "And short-ish."

"Okay, blue and short-ish," Mom repeats. "We can work with that."

I try on dress after dress, but nothing seems right. There's some vital data I'm missing, but I have no idea what it could be.

As Mom helps me with a zipper, she asks softly, "So what's been going on with you and your sister? It's not like you two to fight."

I sigh. "Why does everyone keep saying stuff is 'like me' or 'not like me.' If I'm doing it, doesn't that mean it's *exactly* like me?"

"I suppose," Mom says thoughtfully. "Unless you're

doing things to please other people. Then it's more about them than it is about you, right?"

"Isn't that what Maisie's doing? Trying to impress all the smart kids at her school instead of being herself?"

Mom sighs. "I guess she didn't tell you."

"Tell me what?"

"Maisie's grades at Hemlock were atrocious. She's lucky she even passed eighth grade."

"Really?" Maisie's never spent a ton of time on schoolwork, but I didn't think her grades could be that bad. All the teachers at Hemlock loved her. But I guess it's hard *not* to love her. At least, it used to be.

Mom nods. "I think almost getting held back was a real wake-up call. That's why she wanted to go to St. Mary's this year—to start over, with fewer distractions, and really apply herself."

Huh. I guess that explains a lot of things. Except— "Why didn't she tell me any of this?"

"Maybe she was embarrassed. I think she admires how serious you are about your schoolwork, Blake. I know I do."

I blink at her. Mom *admires* me?

"Anyway," she goes on, "Maisie's trying to buckle down. That's why she decided to take time off from field hockey. And I think she's discovered that she actually likes this more serious side of herself. That she doesn't need to always be going to a party or on a date to feel confident."

I remember the look on her face when she told us about that A-minus on her math test. She wasn't bragging. She was really proud of what she'd accomplished.

And I didn't understand at all.

The last of my anger drains out of me, and I suddenly feel terrible about the things I said to her earlier.

"My girls are growing up," Mom says. "Maisie's becoming more serious, and you're making new friends and trying new things. That's what becoming your own person is all about."

As I stare at myself in the mirror, I'm surprised to realize that the girl staring back hardly looks like me. I used to think that once my experiment was over, I could go back to how I was before. But maybe it's changing me . . . for good.

CHAPTER 23

The next morning, Uncle Joe comes over while I'm eating breakfast. Dad is still upstairs getting ready. We can hear him limping around above our heads.

Mom and Maisie are already gone, so it's just me and Uncle Joe.

"How are things at school?" he asks.

"Good," I say automatically, because there's no point in trying to explain how complicated it all is. I doubt my uncle would understand anyway, since he gets along with everyone. "You liked middle school, right, Uncle Joe?"

He chuckles. "Does anyone actually *like* it? But looking back, yeah. Those were some of the best years of my life."

"Really?"

"Things were easier, you know? You didn't have to worry about impressing people all the time. Not like when you're an adult."

I want to laugh. "I feel like all I do is try to impress people."

"Nah," he says. "Just be yourself, kid. While you still can. Because when you get to be my age, you start to see all the things you did wrong."

"What did *you* do wrong?" I think about his fancy job and fancy apartment and fancy car. "You have everything anyone could ever want."

"Well, not everything," he says, and there's a touch of sadness in his voice I've never heard before. "I give your dad a hard time, but to be honest, I'd kill to have what he has. You girls, your family . . ." He shakes his head. "You spend so much time trying to outdo everyone else, to prove that you're the best, and it turns out, when all is said and done, all you've managed is to push everyone else away."

We hear a loud groan upstairs, and then Dad starts limping around again.

"Do you really think he'll be ready for the race next weekend?" I ask.

"Maybe not," Uncle Joe admits. "But that's the great thing about your dad. He keeps going even when things get tough. That's why I like having him around."

It's funny. All this time, I wondered if Uncle Joe was pushing Dad into stuff simply to mess with him. But maybe my uncle's just lonely, and I never noticed it before. Maybe being successful and popular doesn't mean you've got everything figured out. Maybe it means you're good at *looking* like you do.

On Friday, all anyone at school can talk about is the dance that night. I thought I'd be a nervous wreck, but I'm actually more excited than anything. This is exactly how I hypothesized that a popular person would feel. They don't stress about social events. They look forward to them!

But when I go to my locker at the end of the day, I have a text from Owen.

Sorry, science club business came up. Can't go to the dance tonight.

My stomach plummets. I stare and stare at the words. His excuse is obviously a lie. What science club business could be so important that Owen would ditch the dance for it?

No. I must have done something wrong. But what? Everything seemed platinum when I saw him at lunch today.

I need to find Kat. Even after everything, she's still my best friend. If anyone can help me figure out what to do, it's her.

Kat is pulling her soccer bag out of her locker when I come up to her. When she sees me, her expression hardens. I guess she's still mad at me.

"Kat . . . I . . ." I try to find the words, but tears start trickling down my face instead.

When Kat sees I'm crying, the fight drains out of her face. "What's the matter?" she asks. "What happened?"

I wipe my eyes and show her Owen's message. "I don't get it," I say softly. "Everything was going great . . ."

In an instant, Kat goes into lion mode. She grabs

my phone and deletes the message. "Forget about him. You're still going to the dance." It's not a question. It's an order.

"What? Why?" I sniffle.

"Because who cares about Owen? Who cares about any of them? Just go with Hector and me, and we'll have an awesome time."

My mouth sags open. "Wait. You're going to the dance with *Hector*? If someone sees you there with him, they'll—"

"They'll see that I'm having a great time!" she cuts in. "And who's going to see me? If Priya is boycotting and Owen isn't going, I bet the rest of the science club will skip it too."

She has a point. "But . . . if you're going with Hector, I don't want to be a third wheel."

Kat rolls her eyes. "You won't. It'll be fun."

"I did buy a dress specially for tonight," I say slowly. Mom would be crushed if I didn't actually wear it. But . . . "I'm not sure I can have fun knowing Owen ditched me. I thought my experiment was going so well, but maybe I was wrong."

"Lily," Kat says, and her voice is surprisingly gentle. "You can't let someone else ruin a school dance for you again. Forget about the experiment for one night, okay?"

I sigh. Maybe Kat is right. I've been killing myself to make my experiment work the past few weeks. I guess I *could* take a night off. And without Queen Courtenay to worry about, maybe Kat and I can actually have fun at a dance together!

"Okay. Let's do it."

CHAPTER 24

After dinner, Kat comes over so we can get ready together.

"Great dress," she says. Hers, of course, is hot pink and ridiculous and looks amazing with the newly touched-up rainbow streaks in her hair.

"Thanks," I say, smoothing mine down. It's blue and shortish like I told Mom, and it does look okay, but I still wonder what would have happened if Maisie had helped me pick it out. I tried to apologize after we got home from shopping that night, but she said she couldn't talk because she had to study. She's basically been locked in her room ever since.

"I'm glad we're doing this together," Kat says.

"Me too," I say, but I find myself thinking about

Owen. What is he doing now? What was so important that he had to skip the dance? Maybe I'm being paranoid and it had nothing to do with me. Maybe he really is busy.

Mom insists on taking a million pictures before driving us to the dance. Dad is out doing one of his final workouts before the half marathon, since it's only a week away. He actually seems like he's going to survive the thing.

I ask Mom to drop us off at the end of the school driveway—mostly so she can't pop out of the car and take pictures of us in front of the school, which I'm pretty sure she wants to do.

When Kat and I get to the gym, which has been decorated with streamers and balloons, I spot Hector first, all dressed up. Beside him, looking downright adorable in a purple bow tie, is Parker.

"I hope you don't mind," Kat whispers, "but I talked to Hector and he said Parker wasn't going with anyone, so . . ."

"You set me up with Parker?" I hiss back. Part of me—the Lily part—can't believe my good luck! But the Blake part of me is worried. What if Owen finds out about this? What will he do?

Kat grins. "You can thank me later," she says. Then she drags me over to where the boys are waiting for us.

I could swear there's a sparkle in Parker's eyes when he sees me. "Here," he says, holding out a white flower. "I, um, made this for you." He seems nervous, which makes my own nerves ease a little.

When I take the flower, I realize it's made out of paper. "Wow, this is awesome," I say. "Thanks."

He shrugs. "It's just something I do sometimes."

"Maybe there's some nerd in you after all," I say.

He gives me a bright smile. "Oh, trust me, when it comes to baseball and origami and LEGOs, I'm a total nerd."

"You like LEGOs?" I ask.

"Yeah, don't you?"

"Totally!" I don't know why this surprises me so much. I guess I assumed that Parker liked sports and . . . that was all? Maybe I've been talking to Priya and Owen a little too much.

"So, you, um, wanna dance?" Parker asks.

I glance over at Kat, who's already out shimmying with Hector.

Then I swallow, remembering the last time I dared let my guard down at a school dance. But this is Lincoln, I remind myself, not Hemlock. I'm not Lily Cooper anymore. I'm Blake. And Blake isn't afraid to boogie.

"Sure!" I say.

Parker is a terrible dancer, but he doesn't seem to care at all. He gets super into the music and lets loose. I try to follow his lead, and pretty soon we're making goofy faces at each other as we flail around.

I can't believe how much fun we're having together. And more than that, I can't believe how easy this is. I spent all those months spying on Parker, thinking he was totally out of my league, but he's just a really sweet, normal guy.

As I dance and spin, I realize this is the most relaxed I've felt in a long time. For once, I'm not stressing about what Priya and Owen and all the other kids think about me. I'm not thinking about the Five Factors of Popularity and scrolling through endless spreadsheets in my head. I'm just having fun.

After a few songs, I'm dying of thirst, so we take a break.

As we head over to get some soda, I notice a few kids staring at me and whispering when I pass by. Are they wondering why I'm here with Parker?

Then I realize—I don't really care what they think. Not when Parker and I are having such a great time.

As we sip our sodas, I say, "Thank you for, you know, coming to meet me."

"Yeah, totally," he says. "This is fun."

"And I'm sorry about . . . about the way I've been acting."

He shrugs. "You've been fine. But you might want to rethink how you pick your friends."

I know he's partly right. But also . . . "They're not all bad."

"I know. I was friends with Owen too, once. He's okay, except he can really hold a grudge."

"Yeah, I've noticed that about him." I look at Parker. "What happened between you guys anyway?"

I've heard Owen's version, but I'm curious about the other side of the story.

"My baseball friends were kind of jerks to him when we were younger. I should have stopped them, but . . ." Parker shrugs. "I guess I was too much of a wimp."

"Sometimes it's hard to tell your friends to stop, even when you know what they're doing is mean," I say softly.

Just then, Kat comes over to me. "Hey, I need the bathroom. Come with?"

"Sure."

I tell Parker that I'll be right back, and then Kat grabs my hand and pulls me away.

As we walk across the gym, I notice even more kids staring at me and whispering. But I try to ignore them.

"Well?" Kat says as we're fixing our hair in the mirror, side by side.

"You were right. I'm having a great time."

"I knew it!" she says. "You and Parker are so cute together."

"We're just friends." Although, if I'm being honest, maybe I haven't totally gotten over that crush on him.

When we get back out in the gym, Kat says, "Oh, look. Ashleigh and Jayla are here! Let's go say hi."

I've been avoiding Jayla since the glue prank, mostly because I know Owen and Priya don't like her. But now I realize that it's something else too—I feel bad. It wasn't funny at all, watching her cry that day. Maybe this is my chance to come clean and apologize.

I start to follow Kat, but then I spot an unexpected face in the crowd: Owen's. He and Priya are standing by the door, scanning the gym. What are they doing here? And why aren't they dressed up like everyone else?

A pack of kids pushes past me, so I lose sight of them for a second. When I glance back toward the door, Owen and Priya are gone.

Uh-oh. This can't be good.

I scan the gym for Parker and find him hanging out by the snack table. I hurry over, my pulse pounding along to the music.

But a couple of girls pop up in front of me, blocking

my path. I recognize one of them from my math class. "Did you really write all that stuff about everybody?" she asks.

"What do you mean?" I call over the music.

She shakes her head in disgust. "I thought you were the nice one. But it turns out you're as snobby as Priya."

What on earth is she talking about? Before I can ask, she and her friend hurry away.

A sick feeling spreads through my stomach as I keep pushing through the crowd toward Parker. Whatever is going on, I have to get out of here right now.

"Hey, there you are!" Parker says, smiling. "Everyone's dancing over there." He points to a spot by the bleachers.

A new song starts blaring through the speakers, even louder than the last one.

"Parker, wait. I need to—"

But he obviously can't hear me. He only waves for me to follow him, pointing at Kat and the others.

Parker starts pushing through the crowd, and I

press after him, finally managing to grab his arm. "I need to leave!" I yell.

"What?"

"It's Owen!" I cry. "I think he and Priya are going to—"

PLOP!

A spray of blue shoots down from above, coating Parker's head and face and clothes. A little bit splatters onto my arm.

I glance up to find Owen's face staring down from the top of the bleachers. But he doesn't look triumphant. He looks annoyed. And then I know for sure, he wasn't aiming for Parker. He was aiming for *me*.

Priya appears at his side and says something in his ear, and then the two of them hurry away.

Meanwhile, kids around us scream, then a few start laughing. But Parker seems frozen in shock.

"Lily, what's going on?"

I turn to find Kat standing nearby, her mouth hanging open. And I realize how guilty I look, clinging to Parker's arm, as if I was holding him still so that Owen and Priya could humiliate him.

"I—I was trying to . . ." I stammer. "It was . . ."

"What kind of psycho sprays ink all over someone?" Kat cries as Ashleigh hurries over with a stack of napkins.

"It's invisible ink," I say weakly.

Kat's eyes narrow. "How do you know it's invisible?"

Because I accidentally gave Owen the idea, I think but don't dare say.

"You were in on it, weren't you?" Kat shakes her head, and she doesn't look angry. She looks sad. "You're just like her, you know."

"Like Priya?"

"No, like Queen Courtenay. You say you hate bullies. Well, guess what. You are one."

A teacher finally comes over, and Kat starts to turn away. Then she looks back at me and says, "I'll get another ride home."

When she stomps off to talk to the teacher and Parker, I expect them to point fingers at me, to blame me for everything. But no one even looks at me.

I realize I'm shaking and about to burst into

tears—I definitely need to get out of here. As I grab my coat, I glance over at Ashleigh. She's staring at me with a hurt expression on her face. But when I try to catch Parker's eye one more time, he won't look at me at all.

CHAPTER 25

"Where's Kat?" Mom asks in the car.

"She's getting a ride with Ashleigh," I say. At least, I assume she will.

"Did you have fun?" Mom asks.

I don't know how to answer that. It was fun at first—the most fun I've had in a while. And then it turned into some sort of horror movie that I don't think I'll ever forget.

I have the world's worst luck with school dances. Even science can't explain it.

My phone chimes. It's a message from Owen. *Thanks for helping me make the next video.*

Delete it or I'll tell everyone it was you, I write back.

Then I'll tell everyone what you did to Hector and Jayla.

My head throbs. Those pranks weren't my idea. I barely even did anything. But I was still involved. I can't pretend to be blameless when I knew about them all along.

Why are you doing this? I know Owen doesn't lash out at people for no reason. What could I have possibly done to deserve this?

Priya showed me the spreadsheet, he writes back.

The spreadsheet? What spreadsheet? Wait, does he mean *my* spreadsheet? The one with my experiment notes in it?

And then I remember Priya copying the link and sending it to herself. When I switched projects, I figured she wouldn't bother looking at it. I figured I was safe. Clearly I was wrong.

Suddenly what that girl from my math class said at the dance about me writing "all that stuff about everybody" comes back to me. But how could she . . . ?

It feels like there's a rock in my chest as I pick up my phone again and check my school email. And sure

221

enough, there it is. A message from ScienceOwl, sent out to everyone in our grade right before the dance, with the subject line *Want to know what Lily "Blake" Cooper really thinks about you?*

I can hardly breathe as I follow the link in the email. It's not my spreadsheet, not exactly. Someone—probably Owen?—copied and pasted only my notes about kids at Lincoln and put them into a new document. The initials have been replaced with full names, so it's obvious who I'm talking about.

Owen Campbell isn't as cute or athletic as his brother. Maybe that's why he's obsessed with getting revenge on everyone who's ever wronged him.

Priya Joshi is cold and emotionless. You'd never guess that she really wants to be a pop singer.

Kat Edwards is too stubborn and cynical to ever be popular. She seems to take pride in being an outcast.

It goes on and on. All my private notes, there for everyone to see.

My phone falls out of my hand and lands by my feet with a thump. My brain is spinning. How did this *happen?*

But when I finally manage to take a breath, I realize it's obvious. Priya must have shown Owen the spreadsheet. He got mad when he saw what I wrote about him, and he sent the worst parts out to everyone as revenge. He probably left in the stuff about himself so that no one would suspect the email was from him.

No wonder he ditched me before the dance. No wonder all those kids were staring at me. No wonder I almost wound up with invisible ink dumped all over me! Reading my observations out of context makes them sound terrible. It makes *me* sound terrible, like some judgmental, popularity-hungry monster. Like . . . like Queen Courtenay.

My heart starts hammering in my ears. If the whole grade hasn't seen this yet, they will soon enough. And then they'll all hate me—*Kat* will hate me, even more than she does already.

I don't know what to do. What should I do? Normally I'd look at my data to guide me, but my popularity experiment can't help me now. It's the reason I'm in this mess in the first place!

There's only one option. I need to flee again.

"Mom," I say. "Do you think we could try home-schooling for the rest of the year?"

"What? Why would we do that? I thought you liked your new school."

"I did, but . . ." But how can I show my face there again when everyone hates me and I'm on Owen's hit list? How many different prank ideas does he have written down for me on his phone?

Mom stops the car at a traffic light and turns to me. "Lily, I know middle school is tough. I know there are a lot of changes happening. But you can't keep running away. Mean kids are everywhere. You have to find a way to deal with that."

But what if I'm *a mean kid?* I want to scream. *What do I do then?*

When we get home, I'm surprised to see Maisie in the kitchen waiting for us. The minute our eyes meet, I can tell she knows everything. She must have heard about it from Parker's sister.

"It was an experiment," I try to explain. "I was trying to . . ."

But she only shakes her head sadly and walks away.

And somehow, despite everything else that's happened tonight, her disappointment hurts worst of all.

Dad is at the kitchen window, scratching his head as he peers out at the shed.

"The whole backyard reeks from your experiment, Blake," he says. "And I've never seen so many flies. I'm sorry, kiddo, but I don't think we can do this anymore."

"You're right," I tell him. "We can't."

I flee to the safety of my room and yank out my fancy hairdo and pull off my fancy dress. Then I put on my rattiest, most comfortable pajamas and curl up in front of my computer. I open the spreadsheet that outlines every step of my popularity experiment, wondering if I should simply delete it all. But I can't bring myself to do it.

As I scroll through pages and pages of data, it hits me how wrong I've been.

My hypothesis was all about finding a group of people to keep me safe, instead of finding a group of people I could actually be friends with. No wonder it all went so totally wrong. Queen Courtenay might be safe because her minions flock around her, but do any of them actually *like* her? I think about how they act around her—nervous and terrified. Cleaning up her messes, giggling at her meanest jokes, because they're afraid she'll turn on them. That's not what safety—or friendship—is supposed to look like.

Maisie is the real kind of popular, the kind I should have been aiming for all along. At the pool party, those girls didn't rush over to help her because they were scared of her. They did it because they liked and respected her.

I always knew I wasn't anything like my sister, but at least I had Kat by my side to reassure me that someone *could* like me. Now I've gotten so far from likable, I can't blame Kat for pulling away from me. I'm not sure I even like myself anymore.

In the morning, I send Bree a message asking if she knows what happened after I left the dance. I figure if anyone in the science club might still be speaking to me, it's her. Especially since there was nothing bad about her in the spreadsheet that Owen sent out.

Kat told the teachers that Owen and Priya were behind what happened to Parker, but she couldn't prove anything, Bree writes back.

Did she say anything about me being involved?

No.

I should be relieved, and I guess part of me is. At least Kat didn't rat me out when she had the chance. But the truth is, I have no idea how to feel about any of this.

After breakfast, I gather up the courage to go over to Parker's house to apologize. His sister opens the door.

"What are you doing here?" Maya asks, crossing her arms and blocking the entrance.

"I want to talk to Parker really quick," I say, but she scowls at me. Then I see Parker peering at me from the top of the stairs, so I call up, "I'm sorry! Really! I—"

"He doesn't want to hear it," Maya says.

Before she slams the door on me, I catch a glimpse of Parker's face. He looks as sad as Kat did at the dance. More than that, he looks haunted. It's exactly how I remember feeling after the Courtenay incident last spring.

When I get home, I can tell right away that something is wrong. Maisie's standing in the kitchen, her face frozen and pale, while Mom paces around, talking to someone on the phone.

"What is it?" I whisper to Maisie.

"It's Dad," she says. "He fell off his bike."

My stomach lurches.

Mom hangs up the phone and turns to us. "Uncle Joe's bringing him to the hospital. We're going to meet them there. Come on."

My heart is drumming as we pile into the car. I bombard Mom with questions, but she only shakes her head and says, "I don't know any more than you do, Lily. We'll have to see when we get there."

I don't notice that my hands are shaking in my lap until Maisie reaches out and squeezes my fingers. I can feel her shaking too.

"He'll be okay," she whispers to me.

I nod. Because he has to be.

When we get there, Dad is in surgery.

"He broke his arm when he fell," Uncle Joe tells us. "They have to put a pin in it, but he'll be all right."

Maisie and I cling to each other, our recent arguments forgotten.

"Thank goodness," Mom says with a long sigh. "What happened out there?"

Uncle Joe shakes his head. "I don't know. We were doing a long ride. Everything was going fine, and then Drew just toppled over." He rubs his eyes and adds, "I guess I pushed him too hard."

"He pushed himself," Mom assures him.

But I can tell my uncle feels guilty. That seems to be going around these days.

The doctor comes out to speak with Mom and tells her the surgery went well. Dad is in recovery, and we'll be able to see him soon. When I hear that, I can start breathing again.

Maisie comes over and asks, "Do you want anything from the vending machine?"

"I'll come with you," I say.

As we stand there looking at the chips and candy bars, it hits me how glad I am that she's here with me.

"I'm sorry," I tell her. "I've been a total idiot to you, to Parker, to Kat. To everyone."

If it were anyone else, that probably wouldn't be enough of an apology. But Maisie wraps her arms around me and says, "I'm sorry too."

"For what?"

"You were right about me acting different. I was . . . kind of a disaster at school last year."

"Mom told me the other day, about your grades," I admit. "Why didn't *you* tell me? I wouldn't have given you such a hard time about it if I'd known. And maybe I could have helped."

She shrugs. "You've always been so good at school. I didn't want you to think I was, you know, a loser."

"You? Are you kidding? You're like the opposite of a loser! You're who I want to be when I grow up."

Maisie laughs in surprise. "Which is funny, because I'm still figuring out who *I* want to be."

"Yeah," I tell her. "I guess it's good we both have more time."

When we finally go in to see Dad, he gives us a big smile, though it's obvious that he's still groggy.

Maisie and I go to hug him, and neither one of us

can seem to let go. Mom wipes away tears as she holds his good hand. His face has some scrapes on it and his arm is in a cast, but otherwise he looks like himself. In fact, he looks better, because he's smiling, really smiling.

"I guess this means I can't do the half marathon," he says, and he sounds so happy about it, so relieved. "I don't know what I was thinking training for it. I should have left it to the professionals."

"It was my brother," Mom says. "He pushed you into it."

But Dad shakes his head. "I could have told him no, but I didn't. I went along with it because I wanted to impress him. And now I'll have the scars to remind me how ridiculous I was being."

Of course, this isn't news to us. We know what Dad's always been like around Uncle Joe. But the fact that he can finally admit it seems like a step in the right direction.

"Come on, girls," Mom says. "Let's let your dad get some rest."

When she ushers us out into the hallway, my phone

buzzes in my pocket. I'm surprised to see a message from Kat. Did she hear about my dad somehow?

But I'm even more confused when I see she's sent me a picture of what looks like a certificate. It says: *Honorable Mention in the Mendon Gallery's Fall Art Exhibit.*

I stare at it for a second, and then suck in a breath. Oh no. Kat's art show was today! I missed it!

I'm so sorry, I write back. And I'm not just sorry for missing her show. I'm sorry for the way I've been acting and for the things I said about her in the spreadsheet and for every other misguided thing I've done since school started.

I wait and wait and wait, but she never responds.

CHAPTER 26

On Monday, I have no choice but to go back to school. The first thing I do is go to Miss Turner's classroom and tell her that I'm pulling out of the Science Showcase.

"But why?" she asks. "Your project was coming along so well."

"Because I don't care about composting! It's disgusting. I promised my dad I'd get rid of it. And it's too late to start anything else."

She gives me a long look. "Are you sure about this? If you give up on the experiment now—"

"I'll have no regrets," I tell her. The only thing I regret is not sticking with my original idea.

"If that's how you feel, Blake—"

"Lily," I tell her. "My name is Lily."

Because what's the point of being Blake anymore when my popularity experiment only made everything worse? I think of my spreadsheet. My research and data and information about my classmates didn't exactly get me anywhere. Instead, it blew up in my face.

The truth is, I'll always be a Lily. It was silly to think some little experiment could change that.

After I leave Miss Turner's classroom, everyone stares at me as I walk down the hall. I should be used to it—everyone stares and whispers when I walk around with Priya and Owen.

But this time it's different. These aren't admiring, jealous looks. These are judging glares and harsh whispers.

I spot one of the sixth graders who used to wear safety glasses like mine in her hair. But today, her hair's long and loose like Priya's instead. "Look," I hear her say to her friend when she catches me looking at her. "It's that girl who thought she could use science to make herself popular."

Her friend snorts. "Yeah, right," she says. "A freak like that? It would take more than science. It would take a miracle."

They giggle as I hurry away, my face burning.

I don't bother going to lunch. Instead I hide in the library like I used to do at Hemlock when Kat was absent and I couldn't face Queen Courtenay's lunch-time torments alone. I can't believe what a mess I've made of everything. At least at Hemlock, I had Kat. Now I have only myself. Whoever that is.

The rest of the week goes by in a blur. Everyone avoids me or laughs at me. The only thing I can do is study. My grades haven't been great after all that time spent working on my project and hanging out with people. No wonder Maisie was doing so badly at school. It's so much easier to get distracted when you have a social life.

The morning before the Science Showcase, I convince Dad to let me stay home sick. Mom would never go for it, but she's already at work.

"We can both take a sick day," Dad says. His arm

is healing well, but he's taking the week off work to fully recover.

I really do feel awful. My stomach is clenched in such a tight ball that I might actually throw up.

After Dad sets me up on the couch with some herbal tea, he heads upstairs to take a nap. I snooze for a while too, then open my laptop, intending to watch all the Exploding Emma videos that I've missed lately. I might have ruined my chance to meet her in person, but at least I can watch her blow some things up.

A notification pops up and sends a jolt through me: There's a new video from ScienceOwl, posted this morning. Owen put up the video he made at the dance. Even after I threatened to tell everyone that he was behind the prank, he did it anyway.

I don't want to watch it, but at the same time, I can't not watch it. Owen blurred out Parker's face, but you can still see that stunned moment when the ink hits him. And there I am, right next to him. You can only see my arm, but it looks like I'm trying to hold him in place rather than pull him away. I watch it carefully, trying to find something that shows that Priya and Owen were responsible for the prank. But there's nothing. I'm the only one who looks guilty, so it's a good thing you can't see my face.

At the end of the video, Owen's distorted voice says, "I thought I was done for the year, but there's one more prank I want to pull. Stay tuned for another video tomorrow on how to make ketchup explode!"

Oh no. Kat.

CHAPTER 27

I get to school as the bell for lunch is about to ring. It was tough to convince Dad that I made a miraculous recovery, but I finally talked him into dropping me off.

As I dash through the hallways, kids give me strange looks. I'm running wildly, still in my sweatpants, my hair all over the place. But I don't care if I look ridiculous. I need to get to Kat. I need to stop Owen!

When I get into the cafeteria, I scan the room. Everything seems normal at first. Everyone is eating where they usually do. But then I notice that Owen isn't in his regular seat. Instead, he's lurking near one of the trash cans, his phone discreetly by his side. Clearly he's filming something.

I glance back at Kat and gasp as I see her picking up her bottle of ketchup, ready to douse her French fries.

"No!" I yell as she starts to open the bottle.

But it's too late. Before I can get there, the ketchup erupts. It shoots out of the top of the bottle like lava, spraying Kat right in the face.

She jumps to her feet, the ketchup dripping from her nose. But she doesn't scream. She doesn't make a sound at all.

"Oh my gosh!" I cry, rushing over to her. "Kat, I'm sorry. I'm so sorry!"

Kat doesn't look at me. Instead, she looks past me to where the art teacher has appeared. "Well?" Kat asks her. "Did you see Owen do it?"

Ms. Deen nods. "Yup. I saw everything. We got him this time." Then she strides off across the cafeteria.

Kat smiles as she starts wiping off the ketchup. "Sucker."

"Wait," I say. "What just happened?"

"Owen's finally going to pay for what he's been doing," Ashleigh says, standing up next to Kat.

"You knew?" I ask Kat.

She nods. "I saw his video this morning. I figured this was our chance to catch him in the act."

I whirl around, and sure enough, Ms. Deen is standing over Owen. Whatever she's saying to him, it's making Owen's cheeks flush. Priya is nearby, looking worried, for once.

"What's going to happen to them?" I whisper.

"Ms. Deen said she and some of the other teachers are sick of the science club kids getting away with murder," Ashleigh says. "She's going to try to get them banned from the showcase."

"Banned from the showcase?" I repeat in horror. I think of Bree, Francesca, Ryder, and the other kids in the club. All their hard work for nothing, just because of the things Owen's done.

What about the things I've done? a small voice inside me asks. It was my fault Parker got doused with ink. If Owen hadn't seen the things I'd written about him, he wouldn't have been trying to ink me at the dance. And Kat only got pranked because she was trying to protect me. Those things might not be my fault, but they happened because of me.

Suddenly I find myself rushing over to Ms. Deen.

"We'll see what the principal thinks," she's saying.

"No, stop," I cry. "Please, don't punish them. It . . . it was my fault."

Ms. Deen looks at me like I'm some sort of alien. "Are you saying that *you* made that ketchup explode?"

Not exactly. But it's my fault Kat was targeted in the first place. And I'm the one who gave Owen the ketchup prank idea.

"It was my fault, yes," I say.

"But I saw them do it," Ms. Deen says. "You weren't even there."

Behind me, I hear Kat say, "Lily, what are you doing?" But I ignore her.

"It was my idea," I announce. "All the pranks were. I take the blame for everything."

Ms. Deen seems stunned. She glances back at Owen and Priya, who are staring at me with their mouths open. "Well," she says finally. "I heard rumors that you were behind the incident at the dance."

"I *was* involved," I say.

"In that case, I guess it's time for a visit to the principal."

Principal Valenta doesn't buy my story. I can tell by the way he looks at me with a half smile on his face during my confession.

"You do realize," he says, "that these pranks have been going on since last year? You weren't even a student here."

"I'm guilty," I tell him, and that part is true. I'm guilty of so many things.

He sighs. "Well, all right. If you insist on being punished, we'll do it. How about this: No science club for the rest of the year."

That's fine by me. I was planning to quit anyway. "But the other kids in the club will still be able to take part in the showcase, right?"

Principal Valenta leans over his desk. "Is there any reason they should be punished?"

"No!" I cry. "It was me. All me."

"All right, then." I wait for him to continue listing my punishments, but he doesn't.

"That's it?" I'm not looking to get suspended, but it definitely seems like he's letting me off the hook pretty easily.

"Oh, and we've called your parents, of course."

It's like a slap. Somehow it didn't occur to me that Mom and Dad would find out about this. They are never going to understand.

As I go out to the main office to wait for my parents to arrive, my head is swimming. Maybe this is a huge mistake. Maybe I should have let Priya and Owen take all the blame. But then I would probably feel even worse.

I slump down in my chair, imagining how angry Mom and Dad are going to be.

A minute later, someone sits down in the chair next to mine and a familiar voice says, "Hey."

I'm surprised to see that it's Priya. "Hey."

"Why would you do that?" she says softly. "Why would you take the fall?"

"Because . . ." I struggle to find the right words. There are so many reasons, some of them that I hardly understand myself. "I guess I was trying to be a nice person, for once."

Priya is quiet for a moment. Then she says, "I heard a rumor that we'd be out of the showcase if it weren't for you. So, thanks. I owe you one."

She stands to leave, but I call out, "Wait. Since you owe me, I have a favor to ask."

She lifts an eyebrow. "Yeah?"

"From now on, no more pranks. On anyone."

"You know that's more Owen's thing than mine," she says.

"If you tell him to stop, he'll stop. He worships you."

She sighs. "Yeah. I guess you're right. He's always been kind of a puppy dog."

"Why did you try to fix him up with me if you knew he still liked you?" I ask.

Priya hesitates, but then she must decide to tell me the truth because she says, "I meant it when I said I thought he and I were better as friends. If we got together and then broke up, I was afraid he'd hold it against me forever."

"So you made him hate *me* instead?" I ask.

"You're so much more laid-back than I am. I thought maybe he'd ease up around you. Stop focusing so much on revenge. But I guess I was wrong." She lets out a dry laugh. "Do you know that he's mad at Jayla about stuff she said to him when we were in *first grade*?"

"Seriously?"

"Yeah." She shakes her head. "I guess I should have tried to put a stop to this a while ago."

"Probably, but it's not really up to you. It's up to him."

"But I'll make sure he gets the message," she says. "Truce?"

"Yeah. Truce."

"You know . . . if you ever want to come back to the science club . . ."

"Well, I'm banned from the club for now. But maybe next year." I smile. "Maybe I'll even run to be president so you don't have to do it anymore. In case you want to join the chorus instead."

That clearly takes Priya by surprise. "Interesting idea," she says. Then she gives me a little nod and heads out of the office.

CHAPTER 28

The ride home from school is tense. My parents won't even speak to me. After they met with the principal, they made it clear that we were going to wait to get home and discuss what happened as a family. I guess that means Maisie is going to be there too. Somehow that makes it even worse.

When we get home and all assemble at the kitchen table, there's a moment of intense silence.

And then Mom explodes. "Pulling pranks on people, Lily? How could you do something like that?"

I open my mouth and close it again, not sure where to begin.

"We want to understand. Help us understand," Dad says.

"I . . . can't explain it," I say. "Not really. Some of the other kids started it, and I went along with it, and then—"

"But you can't go along with things because other people are doing them," Dad says. "You know that, Lily."

Meanwhile, Mom is still raging. "Maisie would never, ever, ever do something like this!" she cries.

When I hear those words, something in me snaps. "But I'm not Maisie, am I? I'll never be her, no matter how much you want us to be the same!" I cry. Then I face Dad. "And who are you to tell me about not doing things for other people after everything that happened with the half marathon?"

My parents look at me in stunned silence for a second.

"How . . . how dare you . . ." Mom starts.

"Lily, we are your parents," Dad says. "You can't talk to us like that!"

"You're grounded! No showcase. No friends. Nothing!" Mom adds.

But I'm done listening. I jump to my feet and storm away.

"Come back here!" Mom cries.

But then I hear Maisie chime in for the first time. "Let her go," she tells them. And the strange thing is, it almost sounds as if she's on my side.

That night, I get a message from Kat.

I heard about your dad's accident. Why didn't you tell me that was why you missed my art show?

Wow, I sort of figured Kat would never speak to me again. Maybe there's still a chance she could forgive me.

I didn't think it would make a difference, I write back.

Of course it would.

I'm sorry. I've said it so many times, but maybe this time she'll know I really mean it. *I messed everything up.*

It takes her a minute to respond. And when she does, it's not what I'm expecting. *Do you ever regret leaving Hemlock?*

Yes and no, I write back. I don't miss the daily torture I suffered there, but Lincoln isn't turning out much better. If I'd known what was going to happen, would I have stayed at Hemlock? Probably not. But I would have done things a lot differently at Lincoln.

Kat doesn't respond, so I guess our conversation is over.

As I go to plug in my phone, it hits me that maybe school was never the problem. Maybe it's always been me.

I come down to breakfast the next morning, ready for another fight with my parents. But instead, I find my sister sitting alone at the table, dusted in glitter and wearing her sparkliest shirt.

"Whoa, Maisie," I say. "You look great."

"I figured if I'm going to cheer you on, I need to look the part."

"Cheer me on for what?"

"The Science Showcase. Isn't that today? You've been talking about it for weeks."

"I'm grounded, remember?" I grumble. "Besides, I don't even have a project."

"Well, technically, only one of those is a problem." Her eyes twinkle.

"What are you talking about?"

Maisie grins. "I might have talked Mom and Dad into letting you start your grounding a day late."

"What? Why would they agree to that?"

Just then I hear footsteps behind me as Dad comes into the kitchen.

"Because we realized you were right," he says. "It wasn't fair of me to yell at you for going along with what other people wanted you to do when I haven't exactly been a good role model in that department."

"Dad, it's okay . . ."

"No, it's not," he says firmly.

"We can work on it together," I tell him. I certainly can't blame Dad for messing up when I've made such a disaster of things lately.

"So if you want to go to the showcase today, that's fine," he says. Then he smiles. "After I get back from the gym."

"The gym?" Maisie and I echo.

"I just signed up for a membership," Dad announces. "Have to be careful with the arm, but I can ride a stationary bike, at least."

"Are you sure that's a good idea?" I ask.

"I cleared it with my doctor," Dad assures me. "The half marathon didn't go as planned, but some good can still come out of it, right? Thanks to those workouts with Uncle Joe, I'm in pretty good shape now. No need for that to go to waste."

I suck in a breath, an idea for the showcase suddenly blooming in my brain. "I—I have to go!" I cry. Then I rush up to my room and get to work.

CHAPTER 29

The Science Showcase is like heaven. I walk up and down the rows, gawking at the different projects. Some are really basic science fair experiments, like making an egg float in salt water, but some of them are amazing.

My plan is to dart past Owen's table so I don't have to come face-to-face with him, but when I glance at his project, I freeze. It's incredible.

"Lil' Blake," he says when he sees me staring. "What do you think?"

I'm surprised he's even speaking to me. And I'm even more surprised to see that he ignored Priya's advice. "You used your pictures," I say. "It looks perfect." The poster has all his important data, but it also has Owen's photographs of the animals he's been tracking. The result is stunning. This looks like something a real scientist would do.

"Thanks," he says. He chews on his lip for a second. "You should know, Priya didn't show me your spreadsheet. I saw it on her computer. When I read what it said about me, I kind of overreacted. I'm, uh, sorry." The words sound clumsy coming out of his mouth, as if he's not used to making apologies.

"I should have never written that stuff about people," I say. "I thought I was 'doing science,' but really I was being a snob."

To my surprise, Owen laughs. "I guess I can relate," he says. "Priya kind of let me have it yesterday about my pranks putting the whole science club in danger. It turns out, she thinks I've been acting like an idiot for years."

"So . . ."

"So, I think I'm done with the revenge stuff for now. I deleted the list of prank ideas. To tell you the truth, getting back at people doesn't feel as platinum as you think it's going to."

"Then why do you keep doing it?"

He shrugs. "I guess it's hard to let stuff go, you know? When people mess with you, it kind of changes you."

"Into a mouse or a lion," I say softly.

"Huh?"

"Nothing," I say, shaking my head.

I start to walk away, but Owen calls out, "Oh, and Blake?"

"Yeah?"

"I did like hanging out with you, you know. I'm sorry things got so messed up between us."

"I liked hanging out with you too," I say, because it's true. For a little while, at least, it seemed like we made sense together. "Maybe we're too alike or something."

"Maybe." He chews on his lip again. "Do you think people can change?"

"Yes," I tell him. "I know they can." I certainly have. "Well, good luck today."

He flashes me a smile. "You too," he says, and it sounds like he really means it.

I head off to sct up my pathetic-looking poster. But considering that I threw it together at the last minute, it could be worse. And it feels like the most honest thing I've done in a long time.

A few kids glance at my project as they walk by but don't slow down, clearly not interested. One boy stops in front of my table, his mouth pressed into a tight line of disapproval. He looks familiar, although I don't think I've met him before. Then it hits me that he looks a lot like Priya. This must be her brother, Ravi.

"This is terrible," he tells me.

"Um, thanks?"

"No, really. I've won a lot of these things. You have to look like you at least tried. And judges love graphs. Remember that."

He waits a moment, as if he expects me to take notes or thank him for his helpful advice. Wow. I thought having Maisie for a sibling was tough, but at least she's always supported me. I don't know how Priya puts up with it.

Finally Ravi must decide I'm a lost cause, because he sighs and walks away.

A few minutes later, a judge comes over to my table. "'The Science of Popularity by Lily Blake Cooper,'" she reads off my poster board. "This was your experiment?"

"Yes," I tell her. "It was a disaster."

She raises an eyebrow. "Can you tell me about it?"

I tell her everything, about Queen Courtenay, about Blake, about the pranks, and about the spreadsheet. Then I tell her how it all fell apart, probably because I was asking the wrong question. I shouldn't have asked what makes someone popular. I should have asked what makes someone a good person. Or what makes them the best version of themselves.

"Wow," the judge says when I'm done. "I wasn't expecting a whole story, but . . . it sounds like you got a lot out of this project."

I smile. "Yeah. Despite everything, I guess I did." Because yes, my experiment was a complete failure, but failed experiments can be informative too. They can show scientists where things went wrong and where future experiments can do better.

The judge nods as she marks a few things on her clipboard. Then she keeps going.

The rest of the showcase passes by in a blur. When the winners are announced and they don't call my name, I still smile. Of course I didn't win. I threw my project together in a couple of hours. But next year, well . . . that might be a different story. Priya and Owen are in first and second place, of course, but I'm glad to see that Bree came in third. Maybe there *is* room to have a little fun when you're doing science, no matter what the other science club kids think.

After the awards are handed out, Priya comes up to me. "Nice project," she says.

"Thanks," I say automatically.

"No, I mean it," she says. "I read through your data, and you were right. This *was* a good topic. I'm glad you stuck with it." She lets out something that almost sounds like a laugh. "I didn't love seeing that stuff you wrote about me, but it was true. You're a really good scientist, Blake. Or is it Lily?"

"I think I'm still figuring that out," I admit. "Congrats on winning again, by the way."

She shrugs. "I always think it's going to feel better. When Ravi wins stuff, he seems really happy." She gestures over her shoulder to where her brother is actually signing autographs for some of the kids in the science club.

"Maybe it doesn't feel that great because science is *his* thing, not yours," I say.

She shakes her head. "But what if I try something else and I'm just average at it? What if I never win anything again?"

"At least you'll be you."

Near the end of the showcase, my family shows up at my table. I was wondering what happened to them. It turns out that after they dropped me off, they went to buy me a bouquet of flowers, like they always do for Maisie's games and performances and stuff.

"Wow, thanks," I say when Dad hands me carnations so colorful they make me think of Kat. I wish she were here to see my new project. She might actually approve.

"So, what do you have here?" Mom asks, looking over my poster.

I'm suddenly nervous, afraid that she'll frown and claim it's all going over her head. But I do my best to explain my project, and she actually pays attention through the whole thing.

When I'm finished, Dad flashes me a thumbs-up and Maisie gives me an enthusiastic "Awesome!"

I'm surprised when Mom reaches out and squeezes my hand. "It's so great to see you doing what you love, Lily," she says.

"Thanks, Mom," I say. Maybe she'll never understand my obsession with "science-y stuff," but it's nice that she's actually making an effort.

My family goes to check out the other projects, and I sit down in my chair, suddenly exhausted. But when I spot Parker, Ashleigh, and Kat heading toward me, my heart starts pounding again. What are they doing here?

"Hey," Kat says as they come up to my table. All three of them are dressed in their soccer uniforms.

"Shouldn't you be at the game?" I ask.

"Coach sent us to find you," Parker says. "We need your help."

"One of our midfielders twisted her ankle this morning," Ashleigh explains. "If we don't find another person to play today, we have to forfeit the game."

"And you want *me* to do it?" I say in disbelief. "I only went to two practices!"

"Please, Lily. You owe us," Kat says. "And the other team . . . is Hemlock."

My stomach drops. I don't want to see anyone from my old school—especially Queen Courtenay!

But Kat's right. I owe her and Ashleigh and Parker and all the other friends I turned on. I might have made a complete mess of my time at Lincoln, but maybe it's not too late to put some things right.

Kat holds out a spare uniform and I take it.

CHAPTER 30

When we get to the field, the game's just about to start. I quickly text my family to let them know what's going on. Then I rush over to the bench with Parker, Ashleigh, and Kat.

"I'm glad you could join us," Coach Nazari says.

"I'm glad to be back," I say, and I realize it's true. It was silly of me to quit the team because of other people. Again.

Speaking of. I scan the field and spot a perfectly sleek ponytail. A head cocked to the side in a judging way. Queen Courtenay.

My body jitters with nerves. I do a few stretches, trying to calm myself down. *Hydrogen. Helium.*

"Blake," someone says behind me.

I turn to find Owen near the bench. "What are you doing here?" I ask.

"Our plan is still on, right?"

I stare at him. Is he talking about the prank on Courtenay? "You still want to help me, after everything?"

He shrugs. "You kept up your end of the bargain. I'll keep up mine."

He's holding the bag I gave him last week, full of bottles of homemade slime. The plan is for Owen to sneak over to the Hemlock team's bench with a water bottle that's identical to the one Courtenay always uses. When no one's looking, he'll switch them out. Next time Courtenay goes to douse her face with water, she'll get a spray of slime instead. It won't hurt her or scar her for life, but it'll show her that she's not safe. Not anymore. Maybe not ever again.

After everything she's done, Queen Courtenay ~~~ves a little payback. Doesn't she? But as I watch ~~to the field, it doesn't feel like the right

"Watch for my signal," I tell Owen. Then I hurry over to the rest of my team.

Coach Nazari gives us a little pep talk before the whistle blows. Since there are only eleven of us today, we all need to play the entire game. Hemlock's team is a lot bigger than ours, so they can save their best players for later. I'm relieved that Courtenay isn't on the field yet, and she seems too distracted yelling at her teammates to notice me. If I'm lucky, maybe we'll get through the whole game without her even realizing I'm here.

Later in the first half, I spot my parents in the crowd and Maisie a few rows back, sitting with some friends. She laughs and chats with them like she did at the pool party we went to over the summer. Maybe that part of her isn't gone after all. She's just figured out how to balance it with her more serious side.

At halftime, the game is tied at zero. I watch as the Hemlock coach waves Courtenay off the bench. She picks up her hot-pink water bottle and sprays water in her mouth and on her face. Then she starts stretching, getting ready to go out onto the field.

I get into position, keeping an eye on Courtenay as she trots to the net. Of course she's the goalie. She probably loves picking the ball up and chucking it at people. Luckily I'm safely on the other side of the field.

The second half starts, and at first, everything goes great. The Hemlock team is technically better than us, but they also clearly don't think we're much of a threat. I can tell they're not trying very hard, figuring they already have us beat. A few minutes in, I watch with satisfaction as my team scores a goal, the ball sailing past Queen Courtenay into the net. I might be too far away to see her face, but I can tell she's furious. On the sidelines, I hear her father yelling at her to get her "head in the game."

After that, Hemlock starts playing more aggressively, and they manage to score a goal too, so now we're tied. Suddenly the elbows come out, and Hemlock starts playing dirty. Just when it looks like Ashleigh score another goal, she gets clobbered by one of ⸱ids. We all gasp as Ashleigh falls to the shoulder. I hold my breath as

Coach Nazari leads her off the field. Oh no. We're missing one of our forwards.

Ashleigh insists she's fine, but Coach shakes his head. "Cooper," he says to me. "You and Ashleigh switch positions."

"What? But I've never played forward."

"You'll do great," he assures me. Then he sends us all back out onto the field.

I walk over as slowly as possible to take my new position. What am I going to do? Playing forward means I'll be right by the other team's goal. Queen Courtenay will see me for sure.

"Come on," Kat says, coming up beside me. "Let's do this."

I take a deep breath. Okay. If Kat's by my side, I'll be fine.

The game starts back up, and I can tell the instant Courtenay sees me. "What are you doing here, Flat Face?" she calls from the goal. "I didn't know they let losers on the Lincoln team."

"They obviously do at Hemlock," Kat calls back.

I chuckle, trying to focus on the position of the ball

on the other end of the field, trying not to let Courtenay distract me.

"I heard you almost got yourself kicked out of your new school, Flat Face," Courtenay calls after a minute. "Figures. Once a loser, always a loser."

Hydrogen, helium, lithium, I recite as I inch away from her, still keeping an eye on the ball.

"Is it true your sister is so dumb, she almost flunked out of eighth grade?" Courtenay calls.

I freeze. It's one thing to make fun of me. But to make fun of my sister? No way.

I whirl around, ready to yell at her, ready to scream. But then I hear someone calling my name. *Both* of my names.

"Blake!" Parker cries.

"Lily!" Kat hollers.

I turn to find Parker barreling toward me with the ball.

Everything slows down as he passes it to me. I glance over my shoulder, and the goal is so close. I turn and start running with the ball. I weave around one of the Hemlock kids. And as I go, I realize I'm shouting.

"Hydrogen! Helium!" I cry as I charge at Queen Courtenay. "Lithium! Beryllium! *Boron!*" I wind up my leg and kick the ball at the goal as hard as I can.

It sails through the air—and smashes right into Queen Courtenay's stomach. Then it bounces off and lands on the grass next to the goalpost.

The crowd gasps and then groans. No goal.

I stand there, stunned to see Queen Courtenay holding her middle, doubled over. From the sidelines, her father is screaming at her. Not to see if she's all right, but telling her to "toughen up" and "pull it together." Exactly the kind of stuff she would always yell at me after she'd clobber me in the face with the ball.

Before I know it, I'm rushing over to her. "Are you okay?" I ask.

"Do I look okay?" she shoots back. I realize that she's crying. I've never seen Queen Courtenay look anything but totally in control.

I should feel victorious for finally getting my revenge. But instead, I just feel terrible.

In the stands, Owen is still waiting for my signal. Everyone is distracted. It's the perfect moment to kick

Courtenay when she's down. But that's what bullies do.

"I'm sorry," I tell Courtenay instead.

I can see the surprise on her face. That I would be apologizing to her, after everything she's done to me. But I'm not her. And I never will be.

As the Hemlock coach comes over to check on Courtenay, I hurry toward the sidelines. Owen looks at me expectantly, but I shake my head.

"Are you sure?" he mouths.

I nod. Yes, I'm sure. No more lies. No more pranks. No more revenge.

Then I turn and go back to the game.

After everything, the game ends on a tie. But my team hugs and celebrates as if it's a victory. Given how outmatched and outnumbered we were, it basically is.

Kat is on the other side of the field, chatting with a teacher from Hemlock, so suddenly I find myself all alone, left out of the celebration. I guess I deserve it, but it still stings.

I'm shocked when Ashleigh comes over and says, "Thanks for covering for me."

"No problem. I only wish I'd actually scored."

"Next time," she says as Parker comes over to give us high fives. And I realize that I want there to be a next time. If Coach will have me, I can't wait to play out the rest of the season.

I spot Jayla and Hector on their way down from the stands. I was hoping they'd be here, even though they don't look too thrilled to see me. I guess I can't blame them.

"Can you guys stay here for a second?" I ask Ashleigh, Parker, Jayla, and Hector. "I need to grab something." Then I run off to get my bag from Owen. When I come back to the group, I'm relieved that they actually stayed put.

I don't know how to start, since there's so much to say, so finally I blurt out: "I owe you guys a million apologies. But I'm not that great with words. So, um . . . here." I open my bag and pull out a few bottles of slime and hand them out to everyone. "You can dump this on my head if you want to, as payback for everything I've done lately."

Ashleigh raises an eyebrow and Hector looks at

me in disbelief, but Jayla and Parker both laugh.

"Really?" Parker says. "You want us to slime you?"

"Yes," I tell them. "I deserve it. Just please, please, please don't be mad at me anymore." I turn to Jayla and Hector. "And please forgive me for pulling those pranks on you. I was an idiot."

Jayla and Hector look at each other. "Yeah," Hector says. "You were. But since Kat thinks you're okay, then I guess I do too."

"I hate the way slime feels," Jayla says, scrunching up her nose. "So as long as you don't make me touch it, I think we're good."

I give them both a grateful smile. I can see why Kat likes hanging out with them so much. If they can ever trust me again, maybe we could even be friends someday.

"What about you guys?" I ask Ashleigh and Parker.

"I want us all to be friends again," Ashleigh says. "No groups or fights or anything."

Parker nods. "Yeah, that sounds awesome."

"It sounds perfect," I say.

Just then, Kat comes over. "What are you guys doing?" she asks.

"Trying to decide if we should slime Blake or not," Parker says.

I clear my throat. "Actually, um, would you mind calling me Lily? That's my real name. Or maybe Lily Blake, or—"

"Or how about LB?" Parker asks, and the little smile he gives me makes my stomach flutter.

"I like the sound of that," I say. It sounds like a fresh start.

"Well," Kat says, "I, for one, am ready to bust out some slime." She grabs a bottle out of my hand and unscrews the top. I expect her to empty the entire thing on my head. But instead, she dumps it on her own.

"What are you doing?" I shriek.

Kat giggles as the slime drips down her forehead. "I always wondered what this would feel like."

"And?" I ask.

She smiles and grabs another bottle. Before I can duck, she slimes me too.

We stand there staring at each other, slime oozing all over our faces. And then we both burst out laughing.

"This is disgusting!" Kat says.

"Yup." I turn to her. "So . . . are we okay?"

"That depends. Are you really done being Blake?"

"Absolutely. I scrapped my experiment. It's over. From now on, I'm LB. I'm taking the best from both and leaving the rest."

She nods. "Awesome." She clears her throat. "And thank you, for, you know, trying to stop that prank on me. Even after our huge fight. And for helping out the team today."

"I couldn't let you down, even if we weren't friends anymore." I swallow, then meet her eyes. "Are we now?"

"Friends?" Kat asks. "I hope so."

I smile. "I do too." Is there a way to show your best friend that you're never going to betray her again? That you're really a good person, despite all the terrible things you've done?

I hope so. Hmm, maybe there's a formula for that.

ACKNOWLEDGMENTS

Writing a novel is often messy—just like science—and I'm so lucky to have a great team to help me along the way. Thanks to writing friends Kristine Asselin, Patty Bovie, Erin Dionne, Josh Funk, Heather Kelly, Susan Lubner, and Susan Mcyer for endless moral support and encouragement. Thanks to Sarah Chessman for brainstorming help and answering various middle school-related questions. Thanks to Amanda Maciel and Talia Seidenfeld for the amazing (and often hilarious) feedback and guidance, and to the rest of the Scholastic team. Thank you to my agent, Ammi-Joan Paquette, for the boundless enthusiasm and occasional hand-holding. Thanks to my family, especially Ray, my first reader, and Lia, my self-proclaimed number one fan. And finally, thank you to my wonderful readers, who inspire me to always be on the lookout for new story ideas.

ABOUT THE AUTHOR

Born in Poland and raised in the United States, Anna Staniszewski grew up loving stories in both Polish and English. She was a Writer-in-Residence at the Boston Public Library and a winner of the Susan P. Bloom Discovery Award. Anna lives outside of Boston, Massachusetts and teaches at Simmons University. When she's not writing, Anna spends her time reading, eating chocolate, and challenging unicorns to games of hopscotch. You can visit her at annastan.com.

READ ON FOR MORE LB FUN!

Anna Staniszewski

DOUBLE CLIQUE

BEWARE

Nobody said
friendship was an
exact science . . .

wish

SCHOLASTIC

When I get to the cafeteria, my brain is still churning with my Friendship Formula idea. I wish I could start right away, but a scientist doesn't simply jump into an experiment. They need to gather information first. I'll have to do some serious research tonight and come up with a plan as soon as possible.

At our table, Kat is sitting between Hector and Jayla. At first I'm annoyed that she didn't save me a seat. But then I notice that the chair next to Parker is empty.

I take a deep breath to steady myself and sit down next to Parker.

To my relief, his face lights up when he sees me. "What's up, LB?"

"Oh. Not much. You know. Stuff," I answer.

Parker smiles as if what I said was actually a sentence. "What did you bring for lunch?" he asks.

"Turkey." I pull out my sandwich to show him. "Turkey," I say again.

"Oh cool. I have ham. But I like turkey too."

A long, painful silence follows.

Gah! Why do things have to be so awkward between us? I might have ruined any hope of him liking me like *that*, but I wish we could at least go back to acting like friends.

Just then, Ashleigh appears. "Hey all! I want to introduce you to Courtenay. She's new."

I glance over her shoulder and almost fall out of my chair when I see the girl standing behind her. I would recognize that pouty mouth and those judging eyes anywhere.

It's Courtenay Lyons, aka Queen Courtenay, aka my nemesis from Hemlock Academy.

No. This can't be happening. It can't be.

Have you read all the wish books?

- [ ] *Twice Upon a Time: Robin Hood, the One Who Looked Good in Green* by Wendy Mass
- [ ] *Twice Upon a Time: Sleeping Beauty, the One Who Took the Really Long Nap* by Wendy Mass
- [ ] *Blizzard Besties* by Yamile Saied Méndez
- [ ] *Random Acts of Kittens* by Yamile Saied Méndez
- [ ] *Wish Upon a Stray* by Yamile Saied Méndez
- [ ] *Playing Cupid* by Jenny Meyerhoff
- [ ] *Cake Pop Crush* by Suzanne Nelson
- [ ] *Macarons at Midnight* by Suzanne Nelson
- [ ] *Hot Cocoa Hearts* by Suzanne Nelson
- [ ] *You're Bacon Me Crazy* by Suzanne Nelson
- [ ] *Donut Go Breaking My Heart* by Suzanne Nelson
- [ ] *Sundae My Prince Will Come* by Suzanne Nelson
- [ ] *I Only Have Pies for You* by Suzanne Nelson
- [ ] *Shake It Off* by Suzanne Nelson
- [ ] *Pumpkin Spice Up Your Life* by Suzanne Nelson
- [ ] *Confectionately Yours: Save the Cupcake!* by Lisa Papademetriou
- [ ] *My Secret Guide to Paris* by Lisa Schroeder
- [ ] *Sealed with a Secret* by Lisa Schroeder
- [ ] *Switched at Birthday* by Natalie Standiford
- [ ] *The Only Girl in School* by Natalie Standiford
- [ ] *Once Upon a Cruise* by Anna Staniszewski
- [ ] *Clique Here* by Anna Staniszewski
- [ ] *Deep Down Popular* by Phoebe Stone
- [ ] *Meow or Never* by Jazz Taylor
- [ ] *Revenge of the Flower Girls* by Jennifer Ziegler
- [ ] *Revenge of the Angels* by Jennifer Ziegler

Read the latest wish books!

shake it off

pumpkin spice up your life

TWICE UPON A TIME
Robin Hood
WANTED
The One Who Looked Good in Green
WENDY MASS

ANGELA CERVANTES

LETY OUT LOUD

the love pug

j.j. howard

girls just wanna have pugs

j.j. howard

alpaca my bags

Jenny Goebel

YAMILE SAIED MÉNDEZ

Random Acts of Kittens

Wish UPON A Stray

YAMILE SAIED MÉNDEZ

meow or never

Anna Staniszewski

CLIQUE HERE

■SCHOLASTIC

scholastic.com/wish

WISHSUM21